Don't Tell My Heart It Can Heal

Hatfield Falls (Don't Tell) Book 2

Annilee Nelson

Leenie B Books
Halifax

ISBNs: 978-1-990607-11-0 (ebook); 978-1-990607-12-7 (paperback); 978-1-990607-13-4 (large print)

www.leeniebbooks.com

www.annileenelson.com

About Hatfield Falls

WELCOME TO HATFIELD FALLS, an imaginary town set in the beautiful province of Nova Scotia, Canada. This series focuses on several individuals in that town who are related by blood and/or their connections at Hatfield Falls Christian Church.

Faith, hope, and love flow here in great streams and small trickles. However, these streams don't take happy easy paths. Instead, they swerve around obstacles, dredge up memories from the past, cascade over plans for the present, and push the characters of Hatfield Falls forward into a future that is firmly rooted in grace and grounded in Christ.

Chapter 1

TRISH THOMPSON MOVED HER gold clutch from the chair next to her to the table so that Brandon Bennett could sit down.

This was the only empty table in a corner that she could find. She had had her fill of pleasant, though mundane, conversations, during which she was constantly on edge that she would say or do something wrong. That was the problem with church events – even weddings – they were often attended by church people, and church people were some of the cruelest in her experience. They ranked just below family on her list of people not to trust.

However, she was discovering that there were at least a few at the Hatfield Falls church who might just prove to be the sorts of Christians she had been taught about in Sunday School as a child. Brandon Bennett was one of those, as were the rest of his family, including the newest Bennett – as of an hour ago – who just happened to also be her friend and co-worker, Lacey.

Brandon focussed the lens of his camera on her. "You should wear that colour, whatever it's called, more often."

"Blue?" Trish pasted on what she hoped was a pretty smile and waited for the click. She and Brandon had become good friends quite easily after meeting at an apple orchard at Thanksgiving two and a half months ago.

"I know it's blue," he retorted. "I just don't know what particular shade of blue it is."

"I would say the shade is dark."

Brandon lowered his camera. "You know you could just say, 'I don't want my picture taken.' You don't have to become sarcastic."

"It's not the pictures." Trish leaned back in the chair and nursed her third goblet of cranberry punch. "It's weddings. Not just this one. All of them. I'm pretty sure Hollywood will be making a movie about me soon with the number of bridesmaid dresses I seem to be collecting." Although it had been over two years since she had worn that last one, which also happened to be the last time any of her former *friends* had spoken to her.

"You can't possibly have twenty-seven of them yet." Brandon removed his camera from around his neck and placed it on the table next to Trish's clutch.

"I think this one makes ten. Well, technically, they're not all bridesmaid dresses. Several of them are flower girl frocks."

"How do you get asked to be in so many weddings?"

"Why? Are you looking to collect bowties and tuxedos?"

"The tux is rented, and no. I'd like to know what not to do." He pulled at the piece of fabric tied in a barrel knot around his neck. "I'm glad Will didn't opt for a bowtie. Those things look dorky. This thing is less dorky."

Trish laughed. She had to agree. Bowties weren't her preference. "That thing is called a cravat."

She thought he and his brothers all looked quite dapper in a cravat and tailcoat. Cravats also perfectly fit the Regency flare that Lacey, who loved all things Jane Austen, had going on with her wedding.

"I call it a nuisance." His fumbling with that piece of dark blue silk was not producing the result Trish knew he was after.

"There's a pin, Brandon. Here, let me help you undress." She glanced around and said that last part softly. They were, after all, in the fellowship hall of the church. Not everyone would find her humour funny or appropriate.

Brandon, however, simply smiled and leaned forward. "If you insist, but just the neck thing."

"Cravat," she said with a giggle. "And I had no plans to take this any further." She shuddered.

"Hey!" he said. "I'm not hideous or something, am I?"

Trish placed the tie pin on the table next to his camera. "You're a Bennett. Of course, you're not hideous."

His lips tipped up at a crooked angle as they often did when he was pleased with something.

"And you *might* be the prettiest of the lot," she added with a smirk. Pretty was a rather misplaced descriptor when it came to Brandon. He was ruggedly handsome with a constant shadow of a beard. Having to be trapped in formal wear was a challenge for him, but he had borne it well for his older brother's sake.

"I am not *pretty*," he grumbled.

"I should say you're not." Henry Bennett pulled out a chair, turned it around, and, straddling it, sat down.

"I'm prettier than you," Brandon shot back.

Trish shook her head. The Bennett brothers were handsome and true gentlemen when under the watchful eye of their mother, grandmother, father, or some other adult who expected them to be mature human beings. However, when they got together with just themselves and a few good friends, they often devolved into junior high boys. Jostling for supremacy in something or other was not an unusual pastime for them – even if that something was being the prettiest Bennett.

"You are both very pretty," Trish assured them. "I dare say it would be hard for anyone to choose the prettiest, unless, of course, you are Lacey. Then, you're both losers."

"But who would you pick?" Henry asked.

Trish chuckled. "Not Will. And that is the only decision I am going to make on the subject of best-looking Bennett." Especially since answering honestly would mean saying she thought Henry was the most attractive, even if she did not want him to be.

"Chicken," Brandon taunted.

"No, smart cookie," Trish returned.

"What are you so smart about today?" Edmund, with his twin, Frederick, joined them at the table. Edmund was the Bennett who Trish had known the longest since they worked at the library together.

"She's not willing to pick a prettiest Bennett," Brandon answered.

"That's easy," Fred said. "It's Emma."

Trish smiled at him. "I like the way you think, Freddie my boy."

"You're not the first lady to have said so."

Frederick Bennett had swagger in spades. Trish liked that about him. He knew his worth and was not afraid to claim it – even if he sometimes did it with a touch of arrogance.

"Speaking of ladies," Edmund said. "How many has Mom tried to push at you today?"

Mrs. Bennett was eager to see all her boys married. Too eager.

"I lost count," Henry replied.

"None," Brandon said. "I had a date." He patted his camera.

"Wish I had had one," Fred said. "Mom had me cornered with Mrs. Morin for fifteen minutes as the woman grilled me about my prospects for the future and what elements of the wedding I had liked most."

"Did you tell her that your favourite part of the wedding would be when it was over?" Brandon asked.

"Nah, I said it was when the door to the sanctuary opened for Lacey, and I heard Will suck in a breath." He smiled as if just remembering that moment made him happy.

"That's so sweet," Trish said.

"Mrs. Morin thought so, too, and Mom had to excuse herself to get a tissue. And that's when I escaped."

"But did you mean it?" Trish asked. "Or were you just trying to get away?"

Fred shrugged. "I meant it. Will's lucky. I bet he and Lacey are going to be just as happy as Dad and Mom are."

"Yeah," the three other brothers said in unison.

"You guys are lucky, you know."

Four handsome faces turned towards Trish.

"I don't think my dad and mom are ever really happy, or it never seems like they are."

"Yeah?" Henry prompted. In addition to being the brother she found most attractive in a way that did not scream brother, he was also the most inquisitive Bennett, and the one she tried to steer clear of the most often. There was something about him that told her he was dangerous for her and her secrets.

Trish nodded. "They're still together, but I sometimes wonder why. There's nothing violent about my parent's relationship like there was with Lacey's dad. Don't get me wrong. They're decent enough people." Unless you were their daughter who had shamed their name. "With Mom and Dad, it's more just two people stuck with each other and not overly pleased to be stuck."

"Perhaps they respect the vows they took."

Of course, Henry would hit the nail on the head with the first swing. It was that perception thing that made her a trifle nervous around him. "Yeah, I know that's it."

"And they might just love each other in a way that is less exuberant than some." He closed his eyes and covered them with his hand as his face scrunched in a pained expression.

"What's wrong with you?" Fred asked.

"Mom and Dad are being *exuberant*," Henry said.

Across the room, Pastor Bennett had Mrs. Bennett wrapped in his arms.

"Aw, I think it's sweet."

"You would," Brandon said. "You're a girl."

"Well, I'm not a girl, and I agree with Trish," Fred said.

"That settles it," Trish said. "I think I am going to change my mind. I pick Fred for today's favourite Bennett brother because he's pretty on the outside and sweet on the inside."

"What is he? A piece of candy?" Brandon teased.

"Hey, don't knock it," Fred said with a wolfish grin. "Girls like candy."

"Indeed, we do," Trish agreed. She could see Henry studying her out of the corner of her eye. She often found him observing her carefully. She shifted uneasily.

"Trish is needed," Cari Welsh, the sister of the bride, said as she and Emma Bennett approached the table. "So is Brandon and his camera."

"I don't have to put this back on do I?" He picked up the corner of his cravat.

"No, we only need you to take a picture of the bouquet toss," Cari said. "And then, Will and Lacey will be leaving, so you'll be needed for that, too."

"Take Brandon. You don't need me for any of that." Trish did not need to catch a bouquet that would make her the target of teasing about when she was going to get married.

"I'm afraid we do," Emma said. "Lacey said to tell you that she will not throw her bouquet until she sees you front and center even if she has to get Will and the rest of my brothers to carry you to your spot."

Edmund laughed. "Looks like she's got you."

Trish wrinkled her nose. Lacey would know that Trish would try to hide from any sort of romantic tradition. She sighed. "I should have never told her that I don't plan to ever marry," she grumbled.

"You don't plan to marry?" Emma's eyes were wide, but she merely looked surprised and not judgemental.

"Don't let my mom hear you say that," Edmund cautioned.

"What is she going to do to me if she does?"

"Try to change your mind," Brandon said as he stood and offered her his hand. "Come on, kid. We've got duties to perform."

"And Mom would start by trying to pair you two off," Edmund said as he trailed behind Trish and Brandon. "She already thinks there's hope for that based on how much you hang out together."

"I hang out with all of you, not just Brandon."

"So, you're not denying the potential, just the exclusivity of who you hang out with?" Edmund's tone was teasing.

"Trish and I are just friends," Brandon answered. "And that's all we will ever be. I'm not the right guy for her."

"There is no right guy for me."

Brandon shook his head. "I'm pretty sure there is, but it's not me. And before you ask it," he leveled a glare at Henry, "yes, part of it is likely because I haven't been able to move on from Zoe yet. The other part is, well, Trish and I are friends. Just friends."

Trish smiled up at Brandon. "He's right. Even if I was looking for a guy to hang onto for more than friendship, it's not Brandon." She shrugged. "And don't worry; it's not any of the rest of you either. Your mom can put away her poisonous Cupid darts."

"I don't think Cupid's arrows are poisonous," Edmund corrected.

"They are if they hit you at the wrong time," Brandon muttered.

"Precisely," Trish agreed softly.

"I'd agree with that, too," Cari said. "But then, there are Lacey and Will, and it gives me hope that occasionally the fellow gets it right."

"God gets it right," Brandon inserted. "Always." He shook his head. "Can't say I find that easy to believe, however."

Boy, did Trish agree with that! In fact, she wasn't entirely sure how she felt about God and if she wanted to continue to believe in him.

"Where do we deposit Trish?" Brandon asked Emma.

"Right here. With us." Emma Bennett had one of the sweetest smiles of anyone Trish had ever met. She tapped Lacey's arm.

"Trish!" Lacey cried when she turned around, and then, she pulled her into a hug. "I thought you had snuck out before I could say goodbye."

"You'll only be gone a for a week because you're required to be back for Christmas. I've heard Barb say it to you every day for the last month."

"Gran is excessively excited about a new member of the family joining us this year," Emma agreed.

Lacey held Trish by the shoulders. "Do not duck when I toss my bouquet. Let it fall where it needs to fall, even if it is in your hands."

"You don't believe the superstition about it picking the next to marry, do you?"

"Amy and I might have prayed over it for a week," she admitted sheepishly. "Corny, right?"

"Very." But it was also sweet how close Lacey and her new mother-in-law were.

"But seriously, if it comes your way, don't let it hit the floor. I'd rather these roses get to decorate someone's home for a while than be crushed by stubbornness."

"If it drops into my hands, I will tend to it well."

"Good."

"But please do not aim for me."

Lacey smiled. "I won't. I plan to close my eyes, have Will turn me around three times, and then give the bouquet a toss over my head." She squeezed Trish close. "Thank you, again, for being a bridesmaid. I know these events are not your favourite things."

"But you're one of my favourite people," Trish replied.

"That goes both ways, and when I get back, we'll watch some cheesy Christmas flicks together. 'kay?"

"Can we torment the guys with them?"

Lacey chuckled. "If you can get them to agree to it."

"I'll see what I can do. Now, go make Will look complete. He looks like he's missing half of himself." And it was true. When Trish looked at Will and Lacey, they only looked complete together. It was not that they lacked anything in and of themselves. It was the way they loved the other. It just seemed right.

She blew out a breath as Lacey walked away. If only she could someday be part of a pair like that, but she wouldn't be. She pasted on a smile and took her place. Girls like her didn't deserve such happiness.

Chapter 2

Henry poked a finger at the bouquet of white roses and some sort of little blue flowers that was slowly dying on the kitchen island. It was pretty, even if it was soon going to wither and turn brown. He was surprised it had lasted until today without looking completely dead.

Lacey had been thoroughly turned around when she had tossed it over her head and straight into his hands yesterday. He guessed that's what he got for standing so close to the group of hopeful ladies. Of course, one of those ladies was not hoping to catch this bouquet, and she was why he had been standing so near them.

He still didn't know what it was about Trish that captivated him, but something did. And it was something beyond her brilliant smile that seemed too large for her face and her lithe figure that made him wonder if she ate as she should. She was tiny. Short. Delicate. Pretty. And fascinating.

He shook his head to clear thoughts of Trish from it.

"When can I safely get rid of this?" he called to whichever of his brothers he heard coming up the steps from the basement.

"Never."

The brother who answered and came into the kitchen was Fred, who was looking for his second cup of coffee for the morning. Fred ran on high octane, as he liked to say, and little sleep.

"I looked it up online last night," Fred continued. "There are several ways you can preserve it. I'll send you the link." He put his travel mug next to the coffee carafe in which he was brewing his fuel and took out his phone. "Some of them are stupid looking, but there were a couple that might work." He scrolled his apps before tapping and then tapping again.

"Why do I want to preserve it?" Henry didn't want a bunch of flowers sitting around his house forever!

Fred looked up from his phone and gave Henry a lop-sided smile as if the answer should be obvious. "It'd be a great gift for Mom."

Ah, that made sense. Too bad he hadn't thought of it himself. Of course, sentimental gifts were not exactly his forte; that, for some odd reason, was more Fred's realm.

"How do you even think of these things?" he asked. "Preserving wedding bouquets seems quite the departure from rebuilding engines and changing oil and tires."

Fred chuckled. "I'm more than head gaskets and lug nuts. I do have other interests."

"Flower preservation? Really?"

"No, flower preservation is not one of my other interests." He slipped is phone back into his pocket as Henry's buzzed on the countertop next to the bouquet. "I just watch lots of videos online about random stuff, and I like girls, so I figure it can't hurt to learn what sorts of things they like."

"You're a mushy, old softy. You know that, right?" Henry pulled his pizza pocket from the microwave and took a seat two bar stools down from his younger brother. There were worse things that a fellow could be called, but being a softy was again a stark contrast to the guy who Henry had seen help wrestle an engine into a car.

"Yeah, I know. That's why my first teddy bear is downstairs in my closet in a box with a bunch of other sappy stuff." He shrugged. "It has to be mom's genes. I'm sure we all have a touch of crazy in us thanks to her."

The two brothers laughed at that.

The disparity between who Fred was at work and how he liked to hold onto memories and mementos didn't seem to bother him one bit. Then, again, Fred had always been sure of himself and had possessed enough self-confidence to share some with his twin, Eddie. Where Eddie might have naturally hung back, Fred pushed forward, pulling Edmund right along with him. Eventually, some of that confidence had rubbed off on Edmund, too. Eddie was still somewhat reserved and a trifle uptight, but he was comfortable in his skin. And he had not been that as a young child.

"What time is Brandon dropping off his stuff?" Fred asked.

"Around ten. He has to sign the lease at noon."

"I can't believe he's starting a business. He never struck me as the suit and tie sort. Like ever. How will he manage being indoors for most of his day?"

Henry chuckled. "I suspect he'll find a way to be outside more often than not, but you know, as well as I do, that what Brandon determines to do, he will do."

"Not without complaining," Edmund said as he, too, joined his brothers for breakfast before heading over to the library.

He would be working extra shifts this week to help fill in for Lacey being on her honeymoon. However, the library had several holiday closure dates coming up, so neither Henry nor Fred felt sorry for him. They would be dealing with their own extras at work this week because there was only one week until Christmas.

"Meh, Brandon's not too bad. Especially, if you compare him to Will," Fred said.

That was true. Brandon would rumble quietly, become silent, and then disappear into the woods. Will would huff loudly and then start trying to order things in anyone's life who would allow him to do so. Or he would have before he met Lacey. Lacey had a wonderfully calming effect on Will, and from what Lacey's sister, Cari, said, the favour was returned since Lacey seemed less anxious since she had met Will.

"I suppose Brandon's living here means we'll be seeing Trish even more than we do now," Eddie said.

"You okay with that?" Henry asked.

"Yeah, we get along well enough at work. I think we can handle seeing each other outside of the library as much as we see each other at the library."

"It's not like she hasn't been here or at Mom and Dad's a lot with either Brandon or Lacey before now," Fred said.

"Do you think Brandon is being honest about them only being friends? They do spend a lot of time together."

And they had from their first meeting at the orchard. It truly was as if two kindred spirits had merged. Or more likely it was two injured spirits that found understanding in each other. At least, that was what Henry kept telling himself. He didn't want it to be anything more than that.

"I don't know why he'd lie about it." Henry stuffed the rest of his pizza pocket in his mouth and started to clean up his section of the kitchen island. No one wanted to come home and clean up dirty dishes and trash after a long day of work, most especially him. His days were going to be longer than normal this week because the store was embarking on their extended holiday hours.

"Will lied about Lacey," Edmund said.

"And we all know how that went." Henry knew most intimately for he had been the one to be present while his older brother was crying over Lacey breaking up with him. "Brandon's too smart to repeat that story."

And Henry truly hoped that Brandon and Trish were just friends. It was awkward enough liking your brother's friend. Liking his girlfriend would be several layers of creepiness worse.

"She's actually a lot of fun," Fred said.

"You're not thinking of dating her, are you?" Edmund asked.

Fred shrugged and smirked tauntingly at Eddie. "I hadn't really considered it. I'll let you know when I have." He slapped Eddie on the shoulder as he left the kitchen with his coffee mug in hand. But, then, he stopped at the door. "You don't want to date her, do you? I mean, you know her best from work and all."

"Me?" Edmund shook his head vigorously. "Not even a little. Like you say, she's fun, but she's just not my type."

"Reads romances, does she?" Henry teased.

"Well, yeah, but it's more than that and nothing bad. She's just Trish. That's all. She flirts with me, but then, she flirts with all of you, too."

Not all of them. She didn't flirt with Henry like she did his brothers. In fact, it seemed like she tried to avoid him as often as she could. He blew out a breath as he put his dishes in the dishwasher. He found her avoidance downright frustrating.

"Then, it's settled. None of us are going to date Trish, right?" Fred leveled a look at Henry.

"Right." At least, he wasn't right now. Maybe never. Not that he didn't want to date her. It was just that, thanks to her propensity to duck for cover around him, he didn't really know her. In fact, he wasn't sure that even Brandon or Lacey really knew her. She had walls. He could feel it. He just had no clue why she had them or what they were protecting her from.

"I mean," Fred continued with a grin, "you did catch the bouquet, so we all know you're next."

Henry laughed. "I will toss it in the garbage bin on my way to my car if you want to follow that line of thinking."

"And I'll tell Mom." Fred darted down the stairs to the basement of the split-level house Henry shared with his two youngest brothers and, after today, his next eldest.

"You're such a tattletale!" Henry called after him.

"What are you going to do with the bouquet?" Eddie asked from his post at the stove. Eddie always started his day with proper cooked breakfast food – unlike either Fred or Henry.

"I'm not sure, but Fred sent me a link for ideas of how I can make it into a gift for Mom." Henry picked up his phone and opened the link. "Let's see. I can dry them or put them in resin..." he scrolled further. Fred wasn't lying when he said some of these ideas were hideous. "Or, I could make them into a piece of art by decoratively sandwiching them between two pieces of glass." That was probably going to be the best idea. Hanging things were more easily displayed than paperweights made of resin.

Edmund slid the bacon he had been cooking onto a paper towel and prepared to crack an egg into the pan just as the bread he had put in the toaster earlier popped up. "I'd check with Brandon if you're thinking about making it artsy looking."

"I was thinking the same thing." Flowers were nature, right? And Brandon liked all things nature. He also was exceptionally good at framing nature. That was why he had decided to start his own business, so he could do more than help people pick out frames and cameras like he did at his old job.

"I'll talk to him when he gets here if he has time before I leave at eleven. Otherwise, I guess it can wait until I get off work tonight. I just don't want those flowers to become unusable, if that is even possible." Henry knew very little about creating art. It just wasn't his thing.

"Then, you should probably put them in water or the fridge or something. That's what Mom would do."

"See ya in a few hours," Fred called to Henry as he opened the front door.

"Don't run the store into the ground until I get there," Henry called back.

Fred was a mechanic at the department store where Henry was a manager. Henry's area of expertise and management was in the housewares and hardware departments. Sports and automotive fell under another manager's supervision, cashiers and customer service required still another manager, and there was a fourth seasonal and garden manager as well. It wasn't a huge store like some other big box stores, but it wasn't a mom-and-pop operation either.

"I'm going to go grab a shower and then do my Bible study stuff. If I don't see you before you leave, have a great day, and if you can wrestle some of whatever you make for supper tonight away from Fred, could you leave a plate or bowl in the fridge?" Oh, the fridge! Henry plucked the bouquet off the table.

"Sure. I'm going easy tonight with a frozen lasagna and garlic bread."

"Bag of salad?" Henry shoved a few bottles to the back of the top shelf and put the bouquet in the fridge.

"Yep, as always."

"Sounds like just what I'd love to eat at midnight." He laughed.

"I'll put yours in the fridge before I tell Fred and Brandon the food is ready."

"Thanks, Eddie."

"Brandon's room is all ready to just set up and live in. I vacuumed and dusted it last night."

"You did?"

Eddie slid his plate of food onto the island and shrugged. "I wasn't sure if he'd think to do it before setting up his bed."

"I wouldn't have thought of it," Henry admitted.

Edmund had not only gotten their mom's love of Jane Austen in his DNA but also her ability to think through what needed to be done to make things run smoothly in a home.

"Thanks for that. I'm sure Brandon will appreciate it as much as I do."

"No problem," Eddie said. "What are brothers for if they can't look out for each other, right?"

Henry nodded. "Yeah, right."

That was something they had all learned from their father and mother. Family took care of family. *Of course, there is family and then there is family. The Bennett family and God's family*, as his dad would say.

Henry opened a streaming app on his phone as he closed the door to the master bedroom and selected a sermon podcast. There was no reason why he couldn't start his Bible study while he showered, since learning about God's Word was, in Henry's opinion, the best way to be ready to look out for both of the families he was part of.

Chapter 3

TRISH PULLED A TWENTY-FIVE-DOLLAR gift card from the rack and turned it over as she contemplated purchasing it. It was the expected thing to do, wasn't it? You sent something to your parents for Christmas even if you weren't sure that either you or they wanted you to do it, right?

She had not planned to send them anything – not even a card, but seeing the Bennetts so often over the past four months had made her homesick. She just didn't know if she was she homesick for her family or just the idea of a family.

She turned the card over in her hand again. That last thought was likely it. She longed for a family to wrap itself around her no matter what. She put the gift card back in its slot. She would send an e-card like she had done last year. Maybe if she told them that she had been attending church, then, this time, she'd get a reply.

"I didn't peg you for a last-minute shopper."

Trish nearly jumped out of her skin at Henry's comment.

"Whoa, sorry. I didn't realize you were so lost in thought," he apologized.

"Who said I was lost in thought?" she countered as her heart attempted to rein in its wild thumping. Why was he here? Brandon had said only Fred was working today.

"It was either that, or you're incredibly skittish." He smiled his disarming smile at her, and she couldn't help but smile in return. He must have gotten out of a lot of trouble in his younger years by flashing that grin.

"I didn't know you were working today." If she had, she might have gone to a different store to get what she needed, or, at the very least, she would not have casually wandered through Drummonds looking at things.

"I'm not." He pinched a bit of fabric of his shirt and pulled it away from his right shoulder. "Not red." He then motioned to the left side of his chest. "No name tag."

"So I see." She allowed her eyes to scan his outfit – medium wash blue jeans and a beige sweater that was un-zipped enough to reveal a cranberry t-shirt underneath. "Wait, you're wearing a red shirt." She ran a finger along her collarbone under her chin to indicate the shape of the neck to his t-shirt.

"It's not Drummond's red, and blue jeans aren't part of the uniform. Therefore, when you combine all that with the lack of a name tag, it means I'm not working."

"Sorry. I guess I didn't really stop to think about what you were wearing. I just saw you in this store and as-sumed."

"Don't worry about it. I mean, I had just startled you out of your deep contemplation over a last-minute gift. I can't expect you to be aware of every detail of your surroundings after such a traumatic event."

There was that charming smile of his again. Why did all the Bennett boys, especially this one, have to be so unignorably handsome?

"It kind of was your fault, wasn't it?"

He laughed. "If it makes you feel better, sure."

She turned from the gift card rack and moved towards the houseware aisle. "It was good to see you."

His brow furrowed. "That's it. No further conversation?"

That was the idea. She had realized from nearly their first meeting that it was far too pleasant to be standing close to Henry and talking, and the more time she spent with him the more pleasant, and, therefore, dangerous, it became.

"The store closes in," she looked at her phone, "ten minutes." That seemed like a good reason to be scurrying away from him.

"I know, but if you're looking for something in this section of the store, I can assure you that, with my help, you'll be out of here even faster than if I hadn't interrupted you. What do you need?"

She couldn't argue with that. "A small strainer with a handle. Mine broke last night and duct tape is not a long-term solution." Though it had saved her spaghetti supper.

"Third aisle down on our right," he replied without so much as a moment's thought. "So, you're not shopping for last minute gifts?"

She shook her head. "Nope. I have all the ones I need." Which was a larger number this year than last.

"Then, if I may be so forward, why the gift card?"

She cast a sidelong glance at him. "It was just an impulsive thought. It wouldn't get there by tomorrow anyway." And it wouldn't buy her what she wanted.

"A late gift is not a horrible thing."

She took a strainer that looked exactly like the one she had used for years until it broke last night from the shelf. "Sales tactics won't work. I already decided."

His eyes widened. "I wasn't trying to sell you a gift card. Honest. I just wanted to let you know that not everyone would think poorly of you for sending a late gift."

"You don't know my parents." She pressed her lips together and turned away from him and studied the handle of the strainer she held. She hadn't meant to say that. She took a step away.

His hand wrapped gently around her elbow. "Your parents would think poorly of you for sending a present late?"

She couldn't ignore him when he was talking so gently and making her arm tingle by holding it. So she turned back towards him. When she looked at him, the concern for her in his expression was so intense she could feel it. How did she explain this without giving too much away?

"Perhaps not for that," she said.

He gave a quick glance to his right as if checking for other people. There was no one in the aisle with them, but still, he lowered his voice. "Do they think poorly of you for other things?"

Her cheeks felt like they had been set on fire. No one in Hatfield Falls knew about her parents, not even Lacey, and Lacey was the only close friend she had here. Why did *he* have to be so insightful?

"I am very good at keeping secrets," he added in that same soft voice.

She blew out a breath. "Yes, they think poorly of me for other things, but I would rather not talk about it, and I don't want anyone else to know." She held his gaze.

His hand slid down her arm from her elbow to her hand, leaving a warm trail in its wake. "I'm sorry. That has to be hard." He squeezed her hand. "I won't mention it to anyone."

"Thank you. I'm sure it will get easier with time."

"Is it a new thing, then?"

"Two years today." Boy, had that been the worst Christmas E.V.E.R!

"And has it gotten easier?"

Had it? She shook her head. "I don't know. Some days I don't think about it, so maybe that means it is getting easier. However, I don't want to talk about it."

"Right. I'm sorry. I can be inquisitive."

"I know. Your brothers have mentioned that about you a few times." She forced a teasing smile to her lips, or at least, she hoped it looked teasing and not just pathetic.

"I'm sure they have," he said with a laugh before growing serious again. "I don't want to be inconsiderate of your request to not speak about it, but I do want you to know that I care and I'm here if you need anything." He released her hand from his grip. "I take an active interest in the lives of my friends."

"I'm fine."

His replying look was skeptical. "If you ever find you're not..."

"Thank you. Truly. It means a lot to have you, Lacey, Brandon, and the rest as friends. I haven't had friends in a while." She moved toward the central aisle of the store that would take them to the checkouts.

"You don't have friends back where you're from?"

"Not for about two years now." She gave him a pointed look.

"Right. No more questions. You'll tell me when you're ready."

She laughed. She doubted she would ever be ready to share her shameful past with him.

"Or I hope you will," he said. "You're coming to the Christmas Eve service tonight, right?"

"Lacey made me promise I would be there." Will and Lacey had arrived home late last night, and Lacey had sent a text to remind Trish of her promise.

"And then, you're coming to Mom and Dad's afterwards?" he asked as they got into line behind about six other people.

"Again, Lacey made me promise I would, and, just this morning, Barb threatened to rearrange a whole section of children's books if I didn't keep my promise."

Henry laughed. "She'd do it, too."

"Oh, I know." Trish moved forward in line. "She's hidden books on Edmund before."

"Has she?" They took another step forward.

"Yes, your grandmother is a sneaky woman who always gets her way."

"That's Gran."

Trish was nearly to the front of the line already. The store was busy, but things were flowing nicely.

"Which of these do you want?" Henry asked as he opened the door to one of the coolers that were part of the impulse buys display at the front of the store. "My treat." He put his hand on a can of cherry-flavoured sparkling water. "It's kind of a festive looking can."

"That's my favourite."

He grinned. "I thought so."

"How did you know that?"

"I've been at Will's when you and Lacey are there. This can is a familiar sight." He propped the fridge door against his shoulder so it wouldn't slide shut and grabbed a can of root beer, which she assumed was for himself. "Don't leave without letting me give this to you," he called to her when she moved to the next available cashier.

"I won't." She handed her strainer to Linda, an older lady wearing a pair of antlers and a slightly hideous but rather cheery sweater.

"He's such a great guy," Linda said with a smile.

"He is," Trish agreed. "And his sister-in-law would never forgive me if I were to say otherwise. My best friend just married his brother Will." Hopefully, the idea that she and Henry were anything more than friends would come through loud and clear to Linda.

"Lucky girl! I've met Will. Well, actually, I've met all of Henry's brothers at least once. Fred works in automotive, you know."

"Yes, I know."

"He's a real sweetie, but don't tell him I said that. Car guys aren't supposed to be sweeties, or so I've heard." She laughed, and Trish laughed along with her while she typed her pin number into the payment machine to complete the transaction.

Linda tore the receipt from the printer and tucked it in the bag with the strainer. Then, she handed it and a candy cane to Trish.

"You have a very merry Christmas, my dear."

"You, too."

"And come back and see me in the new year," Linda added.

"I'm sure I will at some point."

Linda gave her a final wave before calling the next customer in line over to her lane.

Trish found Henry waiting for her at the door. "You got Linda, huh?"

"I sure did. She's very friendly."

"The friendliest. Customers rarely leave her till without a smile. I understand she's been manning that cash register for fifteen years."

"Fifteen years as a cashier?" That was an impressively long time for a position that most only took as a stepping-stone to another career.

"She says she never wanted to be anything else and didn't need higher wages because she only works part time for all the extras since her husband's job pays well enough for them to live on."

"She seems happy enough."

"She is. She truly is. I know because I asked her once." He winked at Trish. "I'm inquisitive like that."

Trish laughed. "Yes, I know."

"She's coming to church tonight. So, you'll probably see her there."

"Does she attend your father's church?"

"No, she's not a church goer. It's taken me four years of inviting her to things to get a yes." He smiled as if nothing else in the world could please him more.

"You're really into the whole God and church stuff, aren't you?" And yet, he seemed nice.

He returned her can of fizzy water to his bag. "That question begs a proper explanation."

"No, it requires a simple yes or no." She pushed the button on her key fob, making the lights on her car flash and unlocking the driver's door.

He pulled the drink he had bought for her from his bag and handed it to her. "You don't make it easy for a guy to get to know you, do you?"

"Sorry."

"Friends should know some things about each other."

"You know I like cherry sparkling water and have a black-handled strainer. What more is there to know?" She batted her lashes at him.

He shook his head. "A lot, but I'll let you keep your secrets for now, which means I can also keep mine."

Her brow furrowed. What sorts of secrets could a charming and popular guy like Henry Bennett have to hide? The thought was intriguing. Just not intriguing enough to make her spill her secrets.

"To answer your question," Henry continued. "Yes, I'm really into the God and church stuff, but I haven't always been."

"But you're a pastor's kid. Don't you have to be into it from birth?"

He chuckled. "Now who's the inquisitive one?" he taunted.

"It was one question," Trish protested. "And I think I answered at least one of your questions."

He reached around her and opened her car door for her.

Oh, he smelled as good as he looked, and he made a delightful windbreak.

"You don't mind, do you?" he asked with a grimace. "I keep forgetting that some girls don't like guys to open doors for them. Rest assured that I do not think you are incapable of opening a door or some sort of weakling or weaker life form or whatever. It's just that Gran taught me that it was a sign of respect to serve others, and things like opening doors is kind of automatic."

Trish smiled at him. This was the first time she had ever seen the unflappable Henry Bennett look so uncomfortable. "You're good. I'm not one of those girls."

He blew out a relieved breath. "I'd hate to have three strikes against me after only being together for less than an hour." He grimaced again. "Not *together* together. That's not what I meant."

"Relax. I know what you meant."

"Good."

She looked at him expectantly. "I believe you were going to answer my *one* question," she prompted when he began to look uncomfortable again.

"Oh, right. Sorry. I got sidetracked there. Um, let's see. I think the question was if pastor's kids have to be into that God and church stuff all their lives. The short answer is no. The longer answer is that all that God and church stuff has little to do with a person's physical birth and everything to do with their spiritual birth." He looked at the hand that was holding the edge of her car door. "Have you accepted Christ as your Saviour?"

Trish blinked. She hadn't expected that. "Um, yeah, when I was really young."

"In that case, I'll add that the God and church stuff also has to do with our relationship status with our heavenly Father."

Panic rose within her. He was not going to ask her about that was he? She was not prepared to give an answer for her rather hostile relationship with God.

"I suppose it does. Thank you for answering my question." Hopefully, that would put an end to this discussion.

He stood there looking at her for a silent moment. "Since I have used up all my allowable questions for the time being, I guess I should let you get out of the cold and on your way."

Trish breathed a sigh of relief that he was going to respect her wish not to be questioned about things as she tossed her bag and purse onto the passenger seat of the car, before climbing in behind the wheel.

"See you tonight." Henry moved to close her door, but he paused. "I apologize, but I have to say this, and I don't even know why. Call it a prompting of the Spirit." He blew out a breath. "Sometimes the relationship between us and God gets damaged, but it doesn't mean that He stops loving us and won't welcome us back. I know. I've been there. Anyway," he shook his head as if frustrated with himself, "I'll see you tonight."

Trish waited until he had crossed to the next line of cars where she could see his sports coupe parked before she started her car. "If only it could be so easily fixed," she whispered to his retreating form. "But sometimes, some things..." She shook her head. Some relationships couldn't be fixed. Some hearts were destined, and even deserved to be, forever broken.

Chapter 4

THE CAR WINDOWS were beginning to fog, and cold was starting to seep through Henry's coat. The warm glow from the church windows joined with his frosty fingers and toes in begging him to just get out of the car and go in already. It was church. He liked church, especially at Christmas time.

Before Henry could decide to either give in to the demands of his fingers and toes or remain where he was, the passenger-side door opened.

"Are you just observing from here tonight?" Tyler asked as he slipped into the passenger seat.

"No, I'm going in." Eventually. Soon – most likely.

"Before the service starts?"

"Before my mom sends one of my brothers out to find me." As it was, he had already gotten one text from Will asking where he was.

"Good plan." Tyler turned in his seat to look at Henry. "So what's up? It's not like you to hesitate about church, or I should say it's not like the new you. This is more like the Henry from high school. You're not giving up on this Christian stuff and going back to partying, are you?"

Henry shook his head. "No, I'm never going back there."

"You know you can tell me anything. I'm not my brother."

Henry chuckled. He had been best friends with Tyler since their first day in school, and he'd become good friends with Tyler's younger brother a short time after that. However, of the two Reid brothers, Tyler was the least likely to tease, torment, and hold secrets as bargaining chips. Admitting his problem to Tyler was likely the best thing to do.

"It's a girl."

"Oh, do tell," Tyler said eagerly before blowing into his hands and then rubbing them together.

Henry turned on the car so the heater would kick in.

"Do you know Trish?"

"I do. She seems to be kind of into Brandon." There was a note of caution in Tyler's voice.

"Yeah, I know. Neither one of them claim it is anything more than friends." He shrugged. "But who knows, ya know?"

Tyler nodded. "Makes liking her tricky."

"Excessively," Henry agreed. "But that's not the thing that has me here instead of inside with her and my family." He shook his head in utter frustration with himself. "I said something to her in the parking lot at Drummonds, and I'm pretty sure it did nothing to endear me to her. In fact, I suspect she's going to try to avoid me even more than she has up until now."

"Wait? She avoids you?"

He nodded. "Seems that way."

"But you still like her."

"Yeah, maybe not the smartest thing, but it really can't be helped."

"Seriously?" Tyler just looked at Henry for a moment as the heavy silent weight of disbelief hung between them. "Trish is *it*?"

Henry heaved a sigh. He didn't want to believe it either, but then again, he also really wanted it to be true that Trish was his special someone in the world, the woman God wanted him to spend the rest of his life with. "I don't know, but maybe. You know the story about my dad and then Will."

"The Bennett curse – see a lady you like and that's it."

"Curse is a good word." Henry definitely felt as if a curse of disappointment and pain were hanging over his head.

"So, talk to Brandon," Tyler suggested. "Find out what's really up there."

"That's not it – well, that's not it tonight." Though it had been an issue since October. "It's not just that I like her and can't get her out of my mind. It's like God has marked her for me like He did you and Blake." And that is where the fear of disappointment and pain came into the Bennett curse.

Once Henry had turned back to the Lord during the summer after his high school graduation, he had felt God's call to witness to his best friends. He had tried to avoid doing it. They knew his sins. They had helped him participate in those sins. But, he had not been able to hide from the calling. Eventually, both of his friends had come to Christ. It had taken a year for Tyler and a lot longer for Blake, and it had almost cost Henry his friendship with both of them.

He knew how this might go with Trish. He knew it far too well.

"Oooooh. She's not a Christian?"

"She says she is, but I think she's like I was. You know," he turned his gaze from the church to Tyler, "running from God. However, I don't think her reasons are like mine. I truly don't think she's running from God because she wants to fit in and have fun. Something happened to drive her away." There was far too much pain and wariness in her eyes for it to be anything else.

He scrubbed his face with his gloved hands. "Why can't it be Lacey or Mom that God wants to minister to her? Why would He prompt me to tell her that a broken relationship with Him can be restored?"

He just wanted to get to know her and convince her that she should give dating him a shot.

"You're gonna hate me for this, but, here goes. I think God chose you because you know from experience. Your mom and Lacey don't. Your experience makes you the best choice."

Henry allowed his head to thump back against the headrest as he groaned at this friend's far too insightful words. "You're right. I kinda hate you for that."

Tyler laid a hand on Henry's shoulder and prayed, "God, Henry needs you. Give him strength and bless him with wisdom."

"Thanks." What else was one supposed to say when a friend prayed for you to do what you didn't want to do? And Henry had to admit, at least to himself, that it was pretty amazing that the guy God had led him to chase after until he turned to Christ was the same person who was providing him with counsel in his time of need.

"Now, before you decide you'd rather be fish food like Jonah was, I suggest that you and I go face the inevitable. It's better to do what needs to be done now while smelling like a fellow who takes showers and washes his clothes rather than later and smelling of fish guts."

"You do have a way with words," Henry teased. "You won't tell Blake or anyone about what I told you, will you?"

"You know you'd do better if you had others praying with you."

Yeah, Henry knew that. He just didn't want to admit it. "Hating you a little more."

Tyler laughed. "I promise I won't say anything to anyone until you say I can, but I'll be praying. And Henry?"

"Yeah?"

"I know your passion for God and the amazing blessing it can be firsthand. I honestly don't know if anyone else could have reached Blake. I know I kicked against the prodding of God that you brought into my life, but Blake?" He shook his head. "You persisted when others would have quit. You've got this, man. With God's help, you've got this."

Henry turned off the engine and opened his door. "I hope you're right. This time seems even more daunting than with you and your brother, and as you said, that was hard." Likely the most challenging thing he had ever had to do to this point in his life.

"I'll be praying you end up with her at the end of this if it's God's will. You know you don't want to be anywhere but in the middle of God's will."

Henry got out of the car and looked over the top of it to his friend. "I'd really like it if you'd stop being my dad for a while."

Tyler laughed as he closed his door. "You do it to me enough. It's about time I get to return the favour."

That was true. Tyler and Blake often called him Pastor Bennett as a way of telling him he had waxed biblically eloquent on some topic long enough.

"Where's Blake tonight?"

"He should be here soon. He ended up filling in for someone at work, and with Friendly's not closing until five and the clean up of the deli machines that can't be completed until then, he didn't get home until six."

"Are we saving him a seat?"

"*I'm* saving him one at the back. You'll have to face your family without me."

Henry chuckled. "Are you heading home tomorrow?"

"Yep. We leave at eight tomorrow morning, so we'll be there well before the turkey is done roasting. Both of us have work on the twenty-seventh, so we'll be back in the evening on Boxing Day."

"Ugh, Boxing Day," Henry groaned. "While everyone else is enjoying a nice, relaxing day after Christmas, I'll be in the store making sure all the sales items are where they should be and marked as they need to be." And then, he'd be up at a ridiculously early hour the next day to be in the store before it opened to the hoards of crazy shoppers eager to snag the best deals.

"If you're off by seven, come by, and we'll have pizza."

"Sounds like a plan. I can always go for pizza." It was his favourite food at any time of the day.

"Where are you going for pizza?" His mom asked as she greeted him with a kiss and Tyler with a hug once they had removed their coats.

"To Tyler's place on Boxing Day after work."

"Oh, how lovely. So, no dates?" Her eyes sparkled with amusement.

"No, Mom, no dates, and no, I don't want you to arrange one for me."

"Would I do that?" She fluttered her lashes and attempted to look innocent.

"Yes."

She wrinkled her nose. "I learned my lesson with your brother. My matchmaking days are over."

That sounded like a bald-faced lie, and he was sure his expression declared his disbelief quite loudly.

"I did not say I would never give another suggestion or ask about progress," she clarified. "And you did catch the bouquet."

Tyler chuckled. "You did catch it so that does mean you're next."

"Listen to Tyler," Mrs. Bennett said as she waved at someone who had just entered.

"You know that hate is deepening," Henry muttered.

"Just trying to stay on her good side," Tyler replied before heading off to get seats for himself and Blake.

The auditorium was filling up fast, but then, it usually did on Christmas Eve. Little Everly Walker, dressed in a frilly red dress scooted past Henry.

"Excuse me," the child's mother said as she, too, pushed her way past Henry. "Too many Christmas cookies," she explained as she chased after her two-year-old daughter.

Henry chuckled. He remembered his mom refusing to let him have even one cookie before coming to church on Christmas Eve. All sweets were strictly forbidden for him and his brothers until after the service, and then, they were portioned out by behaviour. His mom was smart. She knew how to manage her boys without a lot of yelling and scolding. Not that she never yelled or scolded. She did, though a quiet scolding was more common than a raised voice with her. Always.

Will waved for him to join them. Henry took a look at the row where Will was saving him a seat. Lacey was tucked in close to Will, and Trish was next to Lacey. Henry sighed. And Brandon was next to Trish. That was probably a good thing, he decided as he made his way down the side aisle to the place on Will's left. It meant he was less likely to say something to her that would make things even more strained between them if he was not sitting next to her.

"I was beginning to think you were dodging church tonight," Will said when Henry joined them. There was a note of concern behind the tease.

"Nope, just a little tardy." He leaned around his eldest brother. "It's good to see you, Mrs. Bennett," he said to Lacey with a wink.

"It is good to be back." Her cheeks were glowing a lovely shade of pink as she slipped her hand into Wills. "Although I could do without the cold."

"Did you go somewhere warm for your honeymoon?" Henry asked. Will had refused to tell anyone where they were going.

"Warmer than here," Lacey said.

"But not much warmer," Will added. "We still needed sweaters and coats."

"But we were able to pick up the most wonderful Christmas gift for your mother."

Will chuckled. "I do believe it might make me the favourite. It's that good."

"What is it?" Henry asked.

Will shook his head. "I'm not telling. You'll have to wait until tomorrow like everyone else."

"Ah, come on. I can keep a secret."

"Nope, not telling."

Henry leaned close to his brother and whispered, "Is it a grandchild?"

Will smacked Henry's leg. "How would I even know this soon?"

Henry shrugged. "It is all I can think of that would make you the favourite."

"He's already the favourite because he's married," Brandon said. He shot Henry a questioning look that asked to know what Henry had whispered.

Henry shook his head. "Not in church," He mouthed.

Brandon scowled.

"A baby," Henry mouthed.

Brandon's eyes grew wide, and he shook his head as he chuckled softly. "I do suppose that will be the next thing he out does us with."

"What are you two talking about?" Trish asked.

Brandon leaned close to her and whispered. She darted a look at Lacey and then Henry. Oddly, it was not a look of shock but rather one of sadness, deeper than Henry had ever glimpsed in her eyes before. It arrested his mind and tugged deeply at his heart. What had happened to wound her so greatly?

"All teasing aside," he said, "I am glad to have you both home again and here with us in church." He held Trish's eyes with his as he said the last part. He hoped she understood just how glad he was to have her here with him and his family – even Brandon. She needed this – not him – this community, this circle of friends who cared for her, this place where God could begin to heal her heart. That was far more important than any relationship. Was that not also how God had worked in him to pursue Tyler and Blake on God's behalf?

He sighed. Why? He didn't want to give up the possibility of Trish being his girlfriend. But then, he didn't want to smell like fish food either.

"You okay?" Will whispered as Frederick began playing the first few chords of "Silent Night" on his guitar.

"Yeah," Henry lied. "I'm great."

Will did not look convinced, but that was too bad. Their father was taking the platform and about to greet everyone to begin the service. Whatever Will might want to ask would have to wait until the service was over, and maybe by then, Henry would know whether he should let Will know about his dilemma about Trish or not.

Tyler was right. More prayer than his own and his friend's was needed. He felt so unequal to the task placed before him. In fact, as he stood to sing the first Christmas song with the worship band, he found himself clinging tightly to the back of the chair in front of him to keep from slipping out of this row and the church and back to the frigid seclusion of his car.

Chapter 5

TRISH TIPPED HER RIGHT ear towards her right shoulder and closed her eyes as she enjoyed the stretch it provided to the sore, left side of her neck. She breathed in and out slowly, then brought her head to centre. She took another deep breath in, pushing her belly out but keeping her shoulders still. She exhaled to a count of four. Then, it was time for the left ear to tip towards her left shoulder so the right side of her neck could get something of a stretch, or it might have been better to say it was time to attempt to tip her left ear to her left shoulder. Pain prevented her from doing anything more than tipping her head a little to the left of center. She grimaced as she held her head just at the point where the pain started and did her breathing.

Maybe she needed a new pillow. This was the third time in five days that she had woken with a stiff neck.

Or, she thought as she massaged her neck, she needed a new life – one without a past that occasionally pushed its way into the front of her mind and forced her to drown it by reading or watching movies so that she could sleep.

"You don't look so good."

"Thanks, Eddie. We can't all be you."

Edmund Bennett pulled out the chair at the small table in the library break room and sat down. "No, I don't mean that. I mean you look like you might be sick." He looked at her lunch. "Is that all you're eating?"

"Yes." She picked up her short, turquoise thermos and took a sip. Ah, that was better. Her tongue was safe. The neck stretches had given her pea soup just enough time to cool off.

"Are you sure you're not sick?" Edmund eyed her thermos warily.

"I like soup, and it's cold outside. I'm fine other than a sore neck and slight headache."

Edmund gave her one more appraising look and, apparently, decided to believe her, for he turned his attention to pulling a container out of his lunch bag. "Lacey might have her microwave bag thing with her. That might help your neck."

That was sweet of him, but seriously, it was just a stiff neck. "If I promise to ask her to use it if the pain gets worse can this doctor's visit be over?"

Eddie laughed as he popped the lid off his container to reveal a sandwich made on what looked like pumpernickel. "Perhaps. Did you take anything for the pain?"

Trish swallowed a mouthful of soup as she nodded. "Stretches."

"That's all?" He cocked an eyebrow over a look that said he questioned whether she knew how to take care of herself or not.

"Yes, that's all. However, I have some ibuprofen in my bag if things don't improve." She placed a hand on his forearm where it lay on the table. "I'm a big girl, Dr. Bennett."

He smiled.

"I can take care of myself. I just can't always resist reading a good book in bed."

The skeptical look was back.

"You don't have to like the books I like in order for them to be good." She removed her hand from his arm and went back to sipping her soup.

"Was it romance?" Eddie asked.

She nodded. "I like fairy tales."

His brow furrowed. "You were reading fairy tales?"

"Yes and no." The love stories found in most romance books she read seemed a great deal like fairy tales minus the good fairies and magical spells. "I read a romance, but that's close enough to a fairy tale in my mind." Prince Charmings, a. k. a. guys as good as book boyfriends, were hard to find in real life. Some girls got lucky and found them – like Lacey had – but others, like her, were stuck with the toads that did not turn into handsome and heroic fellas.

"Meh, I don't know," Eddie muttered.

"You don't know what?"

"I don't think romance books are fairy tales. They're fiction, but they're a lot closer to real life than a fairy tale." His head bobbed from side to side. "Well, some genres of romance are. There are some I see come across the processing table that make fairy tales look like nothing out of the ordinary, day-to-day way of life." He blew out a breath. "I don't know how some people can read those things, but they do."

Edmund was a bit of a literary snob. He preferred rather dull and old-fashioned books. The kind that held stories Trish had only appreciated once they were over and she had time to consider in modern English what she had slogged through in the parlance of yesteryear – or until she had watched the movie adaptation. Even then, some of them were tales she would gladly pay to avoid.

"There are plenty of genres that make me think that very thing," she agreed. "I mean, a husband who locks his wife in the attic and takes up a relationship with the hired help? How do people tolerate such drivel?" She hid her smile behind her thermos as she drank some more of her soup.

He simply leveled an unamused look at her and turned his attention to his lunch.

"Actually," she said, "*Jane Eyre* might be closer to real life than some." She swallowed another sip of her soup. "Not the locking the crazy wife in the attic part – the carrying on with the help part."

He looked up at her from his impressively presented sandwich. He always had the best lunches.

"For me, I'd rather read true fiction, a.k.a. romance," she said. "There. I've said it. I read to escape reality and dream of what seems impossible. Despise me if you will."

He chuckled. "I won't despise you."

"No, but you'll continue to question my reading choices."

"And you'll question mine."

That was true. "Is that radicchio?" she asked. There was a bit of red something on top of the orange cheese in his sandwich.

He nodded since his mouth was full.

"Did you make that sandwich?"

"Yep. Last night. I thought it would be a nice change from the mixed sprouts I had last week."

What single guy cared about what sort of garden-y thing they put on their sandwich? None that she had met before Edmund. "You're a bachelor, right?"

"Last I checked."

"And you're not a secret chef?"

He chuckled. "I like food."

"Fancy food."

"Occasionally, yes."

From what she had seen here in the lunchroom, he liked fancy food more than occasionally. It was more like daily. "Fancy lettuce, classic novels. All you need is a large fortune, and you'd have ladies swooning at your feet."

He laughed out loud at that. "Is that all it takes?"

She shrugged and put her thermos in her tote bag. "For some."

"Not that I'm trying to make you swoon or anything," he grinned at her, "but I'm on cooking duty tonight. Do you want to join us for dinner? Henry's working, but Fred and Brandon will be there. I've got Beef Bourguignon in the slow cooker."

"Seriously? Beef Bourguignon? In a slow cooker?"

"Yep."

"Are you sure you'll have enough if I join you?"

"Yeah, I'm sure. We usually have leftovers when I make it, and I'll take out Henry's serving before I let the others near the pot."

"And you really don't mind if I crash your dinner?"

"Not if you don't mind eating fancy food in front of the tv and in comfy clothes. Respectably comfy," he added quickly.

"Sure, I can do sweats and fancy food on the couch."

He sighed and smiled. "Good. Now, I feel better about you only eating soup for lunch."

"It was pea soup – fiber, protein, all the good stuff."

"If you say so."

"I made it myself. Does that score me any points?"

He reluctantly agreed that it did. For being so young, he certainly was set in his ways and opinions.

"I guess those books won't shelve themselves." She tucked her bag into her cubby.

"Unfortunately, they don't process themselves either, but at least, I have a few more minutes before I have to return to my books." He opened a second container. Was that a brownie? Trish wondered if he had made it or if maybe his sister, the baker, had.

"Emma's," he said as if he was reading her mind. "If you're lucky, there might be some left tonight, but no guarantees at our place."

She chuckled. She knew from the time she had spent with Brandon that food, especially sweet treats, was descended upon with a fervour by the Bennett brothers.

"Have fun processing all those romances."

He shook his head and gave her a wave as she exited the lunchroom to make her way down the hall from the break room to the door that would take her back into the main library space.

Stepping into the library, she breathed in the musty, dusty scent of books and listened to the sounds of soft voices from the far left of the library where the study carrels were, and, to her right, the clash of toys being played with. This afternoon, she would be shelving books on her knees amid the din to her right, but she didn't mind. She loved children.

She stopped just inside the children's area and parked her cart out of the way of the few preschoolers who were stacking large foam blocks and pushing trucks around a carpet that was printed with streets and a village. Two ladies, likely moms of one or more of the children who were playing, sat talking in a corner while another breast-fed her baby just to their left.

Trish wrapped her arms around the three books she had pulled off her cart and pressed them to her chest to try to catch and contain the aching that such a beautiful sight brought to her heart.

"Hey, you want some help?" Lacey asked.

Trish pulled her eyes away from the breastfeeding mother. "Sure, but don't you have lunch now?"

"Not for fifteen minutes, and all my books are on their shelves. I can clean out the book return after my lunch."

"Then, grab some books." Trish looked at the author's name on the book on top of her stack of three and moved toward the section where authors' last names beginning with *F* could be found.

"Will and I would like to have you over on New Year's Eve," Lacey said as she took a few books from the shelving cart. "He's inviting his brothers and Nate, and I'm inviting his sister and mine." She came over to where Trish was and knelt down to search for the right place to put the first book. "I think I might also invite Tiffany from church since she works with Will and Nate and then, a couple of other younger single women from the ladies' group." Lacey slid a book into its place on the shelf. "You should come to that group with me. Mrs. Bennett leads it, and Barb is always there." She smiled at Trish. "But no pressure unless we're talking about New Year's Eve. Then, there is pressure, because I want you there."

Trish's heart raced. She had been attending church on the Sundays when she was not scheduled at the library, but sitting in a service with a hundred and fifty other people who only spoke to her in general pleasantries in the foyer was not as anxiety-inducing as being in a small, chatty group of ladies, even if one of them was her best friend and the other was the Bennett's sweet and opinionated grandmother, Barb. Could she do it? Would it require her to *share* things she did not want anyone to know?

"Will you come to our house New Year's Eve?" Lacey prompted. Her face held such expectation that Trish could not refuse even if she wanted to.

"Sure. Can I bring something?"

"Chips, please. Maybe two bags?"

"Just chips?"

"Yeah, just chips and you. That's all we need because Edmund promised to bring some little sandwiches."

Of course, that's what the king of fancy lettuce would bring, Trish thought with a smile.

"Fred is bringing beverages," Lacey continued. "Emma and Cari are bringing cookies. Brandon said he'd bring chocolate, and Henry is bringing pizza because I guess Henry always brings pizza when he's asked to bring something. At least, that's what Will says. Nate insisted on bringing nachos. I will have a tray of fruit and veggies, and we're filling in from there as we invite people."

"That's a lot of food."

"The Bennett brothers will be there so it might not be as much as we think," Lacey said with a laugh. "I don't know how their parents managed to feed them as teens without going broke."

Trish chuckled. "I know my mom always complained about how much my brother, Trevor, ate when he was in high school."

"She still would if I lived at home."

Trish froze. It couldn't be. Slowly, she turned around. Tears sprang to her eyes. "Trevor? What are you doing here?"

"Visiting my little sister." He held out a hand to help her from the floor. "I didn't know where you lived, so I thought my best option was to come here since I knew you worked at the library." He pulled her into a firm embrace.

"No," he whispered as if he had read the fear in her heart, "Mom and Dad don't know I'm here. I just couldn't let you face another new year without some family present, and I miss you."

"I miss you, too." She clung to him and drew a shaky breath. How dearly she had missed him! She and Trevor had always been so close until she had started dating Michael. She should have listened to him about Michael.

"I shouldn't keep you from your work, but I wanted to see you and ask if you wanted to go out for dinner tonight. I'm staying at the motel just outside of Hatfield Falls." He glanced at Lacey when he released Trish. "Of course, you might have plans already."

"Hi. I'm Lacey Bennett, Trish's co-worker and friend." Lacey held out her hand to Trevor, and he shook it.

"I'm happy to hear she has a friend. It can be hard to make them in a new town."

Lacey smiled. "I know all about that. I just moved to Hatfield Falls this year. Trish has been a real blessing to me."

Trish shook her head as she felt her cheeks growing warm. She was a blessing? That seemed to be a stretch. They worked. They talked. They hung out. It wasn't like Trish was doing anything so great.

"It's true," Lacey insisted. "She was even a bridesmaid in my wedding a little over a week ago."

"Congratulations!" Trevor said. "I'm a fan of marriage myself, though I have yet to find a wife."

"What about Becca?" The last Trish had heard, he was dating a lovely Christian girl with "high moral standards." Of course, that last bit of description had been her mother's way of pointing out Trish's shortcomings.

"That was nothing serious. We went out a few times, but she's..." he grimaced. "Let's just say she's not for me, and I'm not for her. Now, about dinner. Are you free?"

For him, she could be free. She turned to Lacey. "When you go for lunch, could you tell Edmund that I won't be able to make it to his house for dinner tonight?"

"Oh, I don't want to make you cancel plans with your..." Her brother's expression was one of curiosity.

"Friend," Trish filled in the blank. "Edmund is only a friend, and one of Lacey's new brothers-in-law."

"Sure," Lacey said, "I can tell him. What was he making? I keep hearing he's quite the cook."

"Beef Bourguignon."

"Wow, fancy!"

"You won't get anything that fancy wherever I take you," Trevor warned. "I'm on a reduced income budget at present."

"I can pay for my own meal," Trish assured him while she wondered why he was talking about budgets. He was a plumber by trade and had always been in high demand.

"That seems rather shabby of me to ask you out and expect you to pay."

"It's not. I don't mind. It can even be my treat."

"Absolutely not! I can barely stomach the idea of you having to pay for your own meal, which I know you're going to insist on doing."

He was right about that. There was no way she was going to let him pay for her if it would put him in a precarious spot. She had spent enough time scraping by after moving to know how difficult it could be. Whatever his troubles were, she was not going to add to them.

Lacey touched Trish's arm. "I'll tell Edmund," she said. Then, she left them.

"Can you talk and work at the same time?" Trevor asked.

"I do it all the time." Trish got down on her knees again and picked up her books.

"I won't take too much of your time," Trevor assured her. "We can talk more tonight, but I don't really want to leave you right now."

His words warmed her heart. She didn't want him to leave just yet either.

He joined her on the floor and sat cross-legged, or criss-cross applesauce as Jenna would always say at story time here in this room. "Do you like Hatfield Falls?"

She nodded as she made a spot for the book she held to fit onto the shelf in front of her. "I do. It sort of feels like my home now."

"I'm glad to hear that. I really am. And, Lacey seems nice."

"She's one of those ladies who lives what she believes – and she does it with kindness." Even when Lacey had mentioned Trish's propensity to flirt rather boldly with Edmund, she was kind about it and even somewhat embarrassed to have mentioned it.

"Are you going to church?"

Trish nodded. "But only because of Lacey."

"So, you just started attending recently?"

Trish felt the gnawing of guilt turning her stomach and sighed.

"Hey, I'm just asking. I'm not condemning. In fact, I haven't been to church in three months now."

"What?" Trish couldn't believe what she was hearing. Trevor had always been a "there as often as the doors are open" sort of person and seemed happy to be that way.

Trevor closed his eyes and expelled a heavy breath. "I need a new place to live, Trish." He looked at her with eyes that echoed her own pain, though, perhaps to a lesser degree. "I'd really like it if Hatfield Falls were that place since then, I'd have you near me."

"What happened?"

He shook his head. "I'll tell you over dinner. This church you go to, is it good?"

"I like it so far, but they have a band and don't use hymnals."

His lips turned up into a half-smile. "Good. That sounds different enough from what we grew up with for me to try it out." He pushed up from the floor. "I've been unhappy since what happened to you. It was wrong. I knew it at the time, but I thought maybe it was a one-time event. Someone being overzealous. A fluke." He blew out a breath. "It wasn't." He looked down at her. "It's so good to see you again. Do you want to meet me at my motel, or can I meet you here at whatever time you say?"

Trish pulled her phone out of her back pocket. "This is where I live. The door to my place is in the back. It's a basement apartment. The library closes at five tonight, and I'll be ready to go to dinner by six."

"You're going to tell me where you live?"

She nodded. "Yeah. I trust you."

He smiled. "Thanks. I know how much that means."

"And Trevor," she called to him as he took two steps away. "Lacey's husband is in real estate – house flips, income properties, development. He's got connections. I'm sure he can find you a place to live and will have some leads on work."

"You want me to stay, do you?"

"With all my heart, Trev. With all my heart"

Chapter 6

HENRY BALANCED FOUR BOXES of pizza on his left hand so that he would have a hand free to open the door to Will and Lacey's place, but before he could do more than get the pizza situated, Emma opened the door.

"We didn't order pizza," she teased and began to shut the door, but Henry stuck his foot out to stop her.

"Hey! You can't have a party without me. At least, you can't have a good party without me." He waggled his eyebrows. "And pizza. You seriously cannot have a party without pizza."

She laughed. "I'm positive that there are occasionally parties without pizza."

"Yeah, but they're not good ones. Now, are you going to let me in, or does Will want to try to melt all the snow with his heat pump so he doesn't have to shovel later?"

His sister stepped back, opening the door all the way. "You sound like Mom. 'Close the door. Your father doesn't want to heat the whole world.'"

Henry rolled his eyes. "What can I say? Sometimes she was right." More often than he'd like to admit.

"She's here by the way."

"Mom is?" He hadn't thought there would be any parents at this party. From what Will had said, it was just going to be siblings and a few friends from church. Leave it to his mom to find a way to alter plans. It was a good thing he had chosen to get a Hawaiian pizza then since it was his dad's favourite.

"Yep, Mom, Dad, and Gran are here. They wouldn't hear of ringing in the new year without their children. Gran assures us it is bad luck to do so."

So it was Gran who had altered plans. That also made sense. His grandmother did not like to be left out of a good time. "And what did Dad say to that? Something like 'There is no luck. There is only God.'?"

"Pretty much."

"Henry's here," he heard Frederick say.

Henry poked his head into the main part of the house. "The party can now begin," he announced and then, he handed the four boxes of pizza he held to Emma, who left him to deal with his coat and boots while she took the food to the kitchen.

"It can't start until Trish and Trevor get here," Brandon said, joining Henry in the entryway.

Tonight, Henry would finally get to meet Trish's brother. He had heard about him from Edmund and Brandon, but he had yet to meet the guy himself.

"Will thinks he has a place for Trevor, and Nate said he could always use another plumber on his list of subs." Brandon leaned against the wall and sipped on a can of cola. "Trevor's gotta be getting tired of sleeping on Trish's sofa. That thing's not very big. I know it's only been a couple of days, but still."

How did Brandon know what sized couch Trish had? "Have you been to her apartment?"

Brandon nodded. "I dropped off a casserole that Mom had made for them. It was all as proper as can be. There's no need to be jealous." He smirked at Henry as he took another sip of his drink.

That last comment hit close to the truth. Not that Henry was going to admit it. "I'm not jealous. Why would I be jealous?"

Brandon cocked an eyebrow. "Why indeed?" He leaned closer to Henry. "Stare much?"

"I have no idea what you mean." Heat crept up Henry's neck on its way to his ears.

"Yeah, right," Brandon scoffed. "I bet you still have my message in your phone from Christmas Eve because I know you don't delete messages."

Brandon had him there. Henry did still have the series of messages that had pinged between him and his brother from the Christmas Eve service when Brandon had caught Henry staring at Trish, and the first one read *stare much?*

"I was just thinking." That was how he had responded to Brandon's first text.

"Oh, I'm sure you were thinking about Trish." Brandon pushed off the wall. "Are you going to wait for her at the door, or are you going to join the rest of us?"

"I'm not waiting for her," Henry shot back. "I'm just hanging up my coat."

"Who aren't you waiting for?" Will asked as he handed Henry a can of root beer once his coat was on a hook in the entryway.

"Trish," Brandon said before he stepped into the main part of the house.

"I'm not waiting for Trish. I was just hanging up my coat," he grumbled and shook his head. Brothers could be such an annoyance at times. Of course, it was likely just God returning to him the bothersome behaviour he had showered on his brothers over the years.

"You two aren't both interested in Trish, are you?" Will asked.

"You would have to ask Brandon, but as far as I am concerned," he looked down at the can he was opening, "no."

"Lacey worries about her," Will whispered.

Lacey wasn't alone in that. Henry took a sip of his drink. "Why's that?"

"Lacey tends to worry about people she loves." He gave Henry a pointed look.

Henry held up his left hand in a defensive gesture. "Not playing and not planning to hurt anyone." Not that he had ever planned on hurting anyone, but he had flirted with enough girls – even made out with a few – without asking them out that he had earned a reputation as a player back in high school.

"Yeah, I know you're not who you were, but even those of us trying to be upstanding guys can get it wrong."

That was true, and Will would know since he had most definitely gotten it wrong with Lacey and almost lost her.

"You know I wouldn't share your secret, right?" Will continued. "If there is one, that is. Is there?"

Henry rolled his eyes toward the ceiling and shook his head. If anyone else had asked him that, he'd have given them a quick no. But this was Will, and he ranked right up there on Henry's list of trusted friends with Tyler. "It doesn't matter if there is," he admitted, meeting Will's gaze. "What she needs is God's healing, not a boyfriend. I just want to see her get there."

Will did not look convinced.

"Ok, so maybe that's not all I want, but it's all I'm allowed to want. So, can we drop it now?"

Will nodded just as the doorbell rang. "Excuse me." He brushed past Henry to open the door. "Welcome! Come on in. Coats can go on the hooks. Boots can go under the bench. Henry can take the chips to the kitchen for you."

That was Will, the guy who liked to organize and tell others what to do. Henry clapped him on the shoulder and pushed him to the side a bit so he could also greet Trish and her brother.

"Hey, I'm Henry." He stuck his hand out to Trish's brother. "I'm going to guess that you're Trevor."

"That's me." Trevor slipped his hand out of his glove and shook Henry's hand.

"And this bossy fellow is my oldest brother, Will."

"I was getting to that," Will muttered, but he did not protest that fact that he was bossy.

"I'll take the chips, Trish. Did you get any good ones?" Henry opened the grocery bag Trish handed him. "Score! All dressed. My favourite."

"You might have to fight Trish off if you want any of those," Trevor said with a laugh.

Trish rolled her eyes and huffed before smiling as Henry had never seen her smile before. He had seen her teasing smirk, her amused slight upturn to her lips, her forced *there's nothing wrong* thin-lipped smile, and the occasional smile she wore when watching a movie she enjoyed and didn't think anyone was watching her, but this smile? This smile lit her face and her eyes and radiated off her. Edmund had said she seemed happier since her brother had shown up at the library four days ago, but this? This amount of happy was something to behold.

"I bought a bag for home," she said. "Just in case." There was her teasing smirk. "It's the holidays and all. We're supposed to indulge a little, right?" She gave Henry a curious look, and Will nudge him.

He was staring again. He grimaced inwardly but smiled outwardly. "Yep, I intend to, but then, I don't always need a holiday to use as an excuse for indulging in the good stuff."

Trevor chuckled. "Yeah, I'm the same, but," he patted his midsection, "more prone to bear the results than some."

"Oh, Henry will just run a little further tomorrow," Will said.

"It's all about balance," Henry added. "A few more treats in means a bit more output of energy the next day."

"You're a runner?" Trish asked in surprise.

Henry nodded. "I like pizza, root beer, and chips too much not to be. But, I'm not just a runner. I also cycle."

"Well, you have that in common with my little sister, too. She likes to jog. Says it clears her head."

"Except she doesn't run in the winter," Trish said. "I have some exercise videos that help me avoid ice."

"You don't go to a gym?"

She shook her head. "I like quiet exercise since that makes it easier to clear my head, and gyms are not quiet."

He could see that about her. She did seem to like to hide herself away from people – especially him. "I go to the one over by Drummonds, since it is so convenient, but I prefer to jog outside."

"Henry works at Drummonds," Trish explained to her brother.

"So does my brother, Fred."

"He's one of the twins?" Trevor looked at Trish. "The mechanic?"

"Yep, that's him," Henry answered. "I suppose if I were to go take these chips to the kitchen, then Will would have a chance to introduce you to the crew inside." He looked at Trevor and then Trish. "I'm happy you both could join us."

"I have a few options lined up for apartments that we can look at on the second if that works." Henry heard his brother say as he headed toward the kitchen.

"So, you did wait for her," Brandon teased in a whisper when Henry passed him.

"Shut up," Henry shot back.

"I'm not going to tell anyone."

"Except Will."

"Meh, you would have told him anyway."

That was probably true, but still, Henry would have liked to have chosen when, where, and how instead of having Brandon force the issue.

"I notice you're not denying you were waiting for her," Brandon continued as he followed Henry.

"Shut up," Henry replied. "Mom, brothers, other people." He waved the hand that held the grocery bag towards the living room and glared at Brandon. Then, the turned toward the kitchen island. "Chips." He held up the bag. "Where do you want them?"

"I'll take them," Lacey said. "I've got some bowls just waiting to be filled."

"I can fill the bowls if you want." He liked to feel useful, and it would get him away from Brandon.

"Sure. I'd love some help." She waved him around the island. "The bowls are by the sink."

"This is quite the feast," he said as he surveyed the numerous trays and bowls of food on the counter. A cooler of various soft drinks was parked at the far end of the island that faced the hall that went back to the bedrooms and bathroom.

Lacey laughed. "I just hope it's enough for everyone. Remember, I've seen how much you and your brothers can put away."

Henry chuckled and put the bag he held on the counter near the sink where two colourful plastic bowls, likely from the dollar store, stood waiting for chips. He squirted some soap into his hands and touched the faucet with his elbow to start the water running.

He was still amazed by how nice this house was. He had seen the mock-up images and plans of what Will's container home was going to look like, but to see it all finished out to Will's and Nate's exacting standards was impressive. It was sleek and modern with a few rustic touches, like live edge shelves, to make it homey and the occasional industrial element here and there to let everyone know that this house was not completely constructed from traditional building materials.

"Hey, did Mom bring her own teacup?" he asked as he spotted a China cup with a green silhouette of a lady on it sitting behind the bowl he was about to pour chips into.

"No," Lacey grabbed the other bag of chips Trish had brought and began opening it. "I have my own set."

"Of course, you do." He should have thought of that. After all, Lacey loved Jane Austen as much as his mother did. That was why her wedding had been on December 16, which was Miss Austen's birthday, and why Will had surprised her with a honeymoon to Bath, England, which was where she had purchased these cups.

"Which book is that one?" He nodded to the cup. He knew that each cup had a quote from one of Jane Austen's books. His mother had read them all after opening the gift that had placed Will and Lacey firmly at the top of her favourite children list.

"Yours," she replied with a smile. "Do you know which novel that is?"

He nodded. "*Northanger Abbey*."

"Very good. Have you read it?"

"Nope, and I don't plan to."

"Would it tempt you to read it if I said it was humorous?"

"Nope. Those kinds of novels are Eddie's thing. I'll stick to nonfiction." He placed his bowl of chips next to hers on the island and glanced at his sister-in-law. He had expected more than a shrug from her. "Aren't you going to ask me if I'd like to watch it? There is a film of it, isn't there?"

She nodded and bit her lip. That was curious. He thought she liked all things Austen like his mom did.

"Is there something wrong with the movie?" That must be it, for she had sounded as if she liked the book.

"It's not completely wholesome." Her cheeks grew rosy. "There's a bit of nudity. Therefore, in good conscience, I cannot recommend it." She wrinkled her nose and squeezed her eyes nearly shut. "Even if I like it," she added in a whisper.

"Ah, I see. I had no idea my mother liked such stories." He popped a chip into his mouth. He'd have to ask his mom about that.

"Oh, it's not in the book. It's just in the movie."

He was still going to keep this info in mind for when his mom began her campaign to get him or his other brothers, who were not Eddie, to watch an Austen film with her. He put another chip into his mouth.

"Hey, don't eat them all."

Henry smiled at Trish and then extended the bowl to her. "Better grab some now, then."

She put a handful on a paper plate next to a slice of his least favourite kind of pizza, and his dad's favourite, Hawaiian. Then, she added a sandwich and three cookies. Apparently, she ate a lot more than he had thought she did.

"Did your brother meet everyone?"

"He did, and now, he and Nate are deep in discussion about some elbow thingy that connects something to something else."

"Ah, yes, the elbow thingy," Henry teased. "It's a very important thingy I hear. The whole house falls down without it."

She leveled an unamused glare at him. "Are you always this annoying?"

He shrugged. "Not always, just at parties."

"And he's well-versed in parties," Brandon inserted. Of course, Brandon was behind Trish.

"*Was* not *is*," Henry retorted.

Brandon shook his head. "Nope, you still know your way around a good time. You just happen to do it sober now."

Trish's eyes popped open, and her jaw dropped as she looked between him and Brandon. Why was his brother sharing all his secrets tonight?

"I was not the model pastor's son in high school," Henry explained to Trish over the hammering of his heart. "However, that is behind me and not something I want shared with everyone." He glowered at Brandon.

"It isn't a secret," Brandon countered. "Nearly everyone knows about it, and I think it's great that you have found something better in Christ."

"Even so, I'd really rather not have my past dragged out. Ok?" Henry slapped a slice of pizza on his plate and headed to the door across from the island.

"Where are you going?" Brandon asked.

"To eat pizza where there are no brothers." He could hear Brandon following him, but he ignored it.

"Hey, man, she needs to know you're not perfect," Brandon hissed after closing the door that led to the breezeway that connected Will's house to his business offices.

Henry whirled towards him. "Does she? Does she really? Or are you just trying to make me look bad and yourself look better?"

Brandon took a step backwards. "You really are jealous, aren't you?"

"Yeah, yeah, I am. There. Are you happy? I'm jealous that you are the one she trusts and not the one she avoids."

He shook his head. What did it matter? It wasn't as if God was going to let him date her. God wanted him to minister to her. Of all the rotten things. He blew out a breath. Maybe this following God with your whole being was not for him after all. Maybe this had been a phase of life, much like his partying days had been. Maybe Tyler was wrong, and he didn't have this. Maybe he didn't really care if he ended up smelling like fish food. Henry took a bite of his pizza, but it tasted bland. He put his plate on the bench near the door. Maybe it'd taste better after Brandon left.

"She reminds me of you. Okay?" Brandon said after several minutes of silence. "She needs to know that there is someone here who might understand whatever it is that she is hiding." He took a step closer to Henry. "And maybe if you stop hiding from your past, it will help her."

"I'm not hiding from my past." If only he could!

Brandon made a huffing laugh sound. "Right."

"Maybe her brother being here will be enough," Henry said to himself as much as he was saying it to his brother. It would have to be. Surely, her brother would help her work through whatever it was, and Henry could just work on trying to get her to not find ways to avoid him.

His conscience pricked him, and he shook his head again. Either way, whether he left Trish to be ministered to by anyone but him or not, he was not going to be able to date her without feeling guilty. And that was no way to start a relationship – if he was ever able to convince her to consider him.

Reality settled on him like robe of iron. It was too much. The weight of what could go wrong was too heavy. The sacrifice of what he wanted for what God demanded was too dear. The image of Blake shouting at him and telling him to never come back flashed through his mind. "I can't do this. You hear that, God? I can't do this."

Brandon grabbed him by the shoulders. "What are you talking about?"

"I know she's been hurt. I just don't know why or how, though it has something to do with her parents. And I know that God wants me to reach out to her, but I'd rather not. I like her, Brandon – a lot – and you know how it went with Tyler and Blake."

"And you know how it is now with them."

Henry shook his head.

"And you know, as well as I do, that it's only that way because you followed God's leading," Brandon continued. "Suck it up, bro, and do what you have to do. You think I don't know what it's like to lose what you want to follow the path you think God wants you to take?"

Henry swallowed. "I guess you do."

"You better believe I do," his brother grumbled.

A knock sounded on the door behind them before it slowly opened.

"Is everyone okay out here?" Lacey stood at the door with Trish behind her.

"Yeah, we're good," Henry lied.

"Are we?" Brandon asked.

Henry bit the insides of his cheeks and nodded.

"I don't care if you have a past that isn't squeaky clean," Trish offered as she stepped around Lacey. "I'd really hate to see something like this come between the two of you."

Henry nodded again while he continued to bite the insides of his cheeks. He just wanted everyone, including her, to go away.

"Do I need to get Will or your dad?" Lacey asked.

"No!" both Brandon and Henry said at once.

Trish laughed. "Maybe their mother would be better."

"Get Will if you think you must get anyone," Henry said. "But seriously, I just need a few minutes. I promise not to ruin the party by storming off."

"And I promise not to tell anyone else about the wild Bennett child," Brandon said.

"You really were a wild child?" Trish shook her head as if she couldn't believe it as she took a step in his direction.

"Sadly, yes. I'm the prodigal of the family, if you will. Not that I had an inheritance to waste, but there was a college savings account that I drained pretty well while chasing what I thought was fun and would make me fit in with the cool kids."

She tipped her head and studied him. Then, she took a step closer to him and lowered her voice. "We all do stupid stuff at times, but at least, you have a family who has welcomed you back." She looked back at the door that connected the space where they were to the house. "I only have my brother."

"And us," Brandon inserted.

"Most definitely us," Lacey agreed.

She shook her head and shrugged. "For now."

"For always," Henry said.

She didn't look convinced, but she also looked like she might turn and run, so he did not press the point any further.

"Yep," Brandon said, "you're one of us now, kid. Might as well accept the inevitable and not fight it."

Trish smiled at that. It was one of those happy smiles she wore during movies. "I suppose there could be worse things?" Her eyes flitted to Henry again.

"Definitely," Brandon agreed before turning to Henry. "I'm sorry."

"Yeah, me, too," he replied.

"Hug it out," Lacey said.

"She spends far too much time with our mother," Brandon grumbled as he gave Henry a quick hug.

"I like your mom," Lacey said defensively.

"So do we, but the hugging thing?" Brandon shuddered.

"Fine, next time, I'll let you shake hands."

Henry shook his head. "Nah, hugs are better. Awkward, but better."

"We're good?" Brandon asked him.

"Yeah, I think we know where we both stand on this."

Brandon smirked. "Yeah, I think we do."

Henry smacked him.

"Hey, don't get started again," Lacey warned, "or I'll tell Will."

Both Henry and Brandon held up their hands in surrender.

"I'll be right in," Trish said as Brandon moved to follow Lacey.

"Okay," Lacey said while Brandon smirked over Trish's head at Henry.

"Is your partying past why you said what you did in the parking lot at Drummonds about you know that God will welcome back someone who has gone astray?"

He nodded. He wasn't going to be able to not follow God's leading, was he?

"But some sins are too great, aren't they?"

"No," he replied with a firm shake of his head. "Nothing is too great a sin for God to forgive and grant restoration."

Again, she didn't look convinced, but she also didn't look like she was about to flee, which was good. "Even if it is more than partying too much?"

Oh, did he know the answer to that. "Yes, very much so."

And there was the reminder of why he had to do what he didn't want to do. God had forgiven him so much, how could he turn his back on God's prompting?

"You know Paul killed Christians. He was even there when they stoned Stephen."

She nodded. Her eyes held his, and it was as if her every fibre was waiting for him to say more. To tell her how she could be restored. How could he not answer?

"And then, there was the Samaritan woman at the well, and the woman caught in adultery," he continued. "Zacchaeus stole from his countrymen, but Jesus brought salvation to his house. And even the thief on the cross was not denied forgiveness when he asked for it. They were all forgiven, Trish. All of them. No matter the size of their sin."

She shifted uneasily and looked back at the door to the house. "We should probably head back in."

"You go ahead. I think I'd like to pray for a bit."

She smiled gently at that. "You really are into the whole God thing, aren't you?"

Yeah, for better or worse, he was all in. He hoped that eventually it would be for better, but there was no guarantee. "When you've been forgiven for as much as I have, what else can I be but thankful and willing to serve?"

She shook her head. "You are so different from what I've known."

"I hope that's not too bad a thing?"

"Not at all." She turned toward the door, but then back towards him when her hand was on the doorknob. "Thank you."

"For what?"

"For being real. Pasts aren't easy to talk about."

"No, they aren't."

"Don't stay out here too long, okay?"

"I won't," he promised.

She closed the door softly, peeking at him one last time before latching it closed.

"I get it, God," he said as he sank down next to his cold pizza on the bench that ran along the wall of the house. "I get it. I'll do what you want – no doubting, no wavering, no turning back whatever the cost – but do you think you could explain Yourself more gently next time?"

Chapter 7

TRISH PULLED OUT OF Drummonds' parking lot. The coffee maker Henry's grandmother, Barb, had been researching all week on the computer at the library had not been in stock. However, Henry had sourced one at another Drummonds store and had placed an order for it to be delivered as soon as possible.

"Will you take me to see Brandon's studio before you take me home?"

Trish glanced over at her passenger. "It'll cost you," she teased.

Yesterday at the library, she had volunteered to be Barb's taxi today so she could do her errands. This morning, Barb had met her with a container of six absolutely delicious peanut butter cookies to pay her "cabbie."

"Peanut butter, chocolate chip, brownies, what flavour payment do you want?"

Barb was known for her cookies.

"Oatmeal raisin."

Barb laughed. "You're in luck. Those seem to be the ones that stay in the freezer the longest. Fred and Henry will eat them, but the other boys aren't fond of them. Now, their father would eat the whole bucket at once if I put it out on a Sunday."

"They've always been one of my favourites."

"See, I knew there was something exceptionally good about you." Barb had turned her full attention to Trish. "Oatmeal raisin is in my top three along with gingerbread and snickerdoodles."

"Ooooh, ginger snaps. Now, if you had those... there's no telling what I'd do for you." She joined Barb in laughing.

"I have a recipe for them." Barb cocked her head. "Marry one of my grandsons, and I'll dust it off."

Trish's mouth dropped open.

"They're all nice boys," Barb continued. Her eyes seemed to be boring into Trish, who kept her gaze deliberately fixed on the road.

"They are," she agreed, both because it was the polite thing to do, and it was the truth.

"But?" Barb prompted.

"But what?" Trish turned off the main road through Hatfield Falls and onto the second most shop-lined section of town.

"What's wrong with them?"

"Oh, nothing!" Trish rushed to assure her. "Your grandsons are all lovely – and I do mean lovely – gentlemen. Any girl wanting to marry well would be blessed to marry one of them." She drew in a deliberate breath. "However, I am not one of those girls."

"You plan to marry poorly?" Barb asked in surprise.

Trish shook her head. "I don't plan to marry." She wanted to marry, have children, do the whole family thing, but it wasn't in her future.

"I don't think Lacey planned on it either when I first met her," Barb countered. "In fact, she told me shortly after I first met her that she wasn't even looking for a boyfriend."

"I'm not Lacey."

"No, no, you're not, but plans can change."

"Not for me." Which, the more time she spent with Lacey and the Bennetts, was a fact that was becoming harder and harder to accept. She wanted what Lacey had, and after New Year's Eve, there was no doubt left in her mind about which Bennett brother she'd pick over any other guy in the world if she were the marrying type. However, Henry deserved someone better than she was. He had his own past to overcome. He certainly didn't need hers added to it. And she didn't deserve happiness after having been the source of such unhappiness in the lives of others.

Barb reached over and patted Trish's leg. "God might have different plans."

"I doubt it," Trish muttered. She had been thinking about what Henry had said about forgiveness, and though she didn't really want to admit to herself, she knew he was right. God could and would forgive even her errors if she asked Him to. However, she wasn't God, and she wasn't sure she could forgive herself. If only she had listened to Trevor about Michael!

She switched on her turn signal and waited for a pickup and a minivan to pass by before crossing over the lane of opposing traffic and into a small alley. "We'll go in from the back" she explained to Barb. "The parking will be easier."

"You and Brandon seem to get along quite well."

Trish shook her head. Barb was persistent. "We're just friends, and I don't mean how Lacey and Will were just friends but were actually secretly dating." She pulled into one of the parking spots behind Brandon's studio. "Besides, even if I did like him in that way – which I don't – he's not ready to date anyone, and I'm unavailable."

"I thought you didn't have a boyfriend."

"I don't."

"Then, you're available."

Trish turned to Barb and cocked an eyebrow but didn't get any further than opening her mouth before Barb added, "to whatever plan God has for you."

"Nice save, lady."

Barb grinned. "And maybe one of my grandsons is God's plan."

"And you just lost that save. I'm not available for anyone, even one of your gorgeous grandsons. I'm just not." The two ladies locked eyes for a full minute before Barb looked away.

"You sure do have some fire in you for being such a little thing," Barb said as she started to open her door.

"Let me get your walker for you before you get out."

"I like that about you, you know – your fire," Barb called to her as she went around to the hatch and opened it to get Barb's walker. "I like that about Lacey, too. My grandsons need wives with spine, except maybe Brandon. He might do well with a gentler sort of girl."

"It's not happening, Barb."

"Oh, I heard you," she muttered. "I'm not happy to accept your answer, but I will. Not that I won't pray for you to change your mind."

Trish unfolded the walker next to the passenger side door and offered a hand to help Barb out of the car.

"Thank you, dear," she said as she accepted Trish's help.

"I'll get your purse," Trish offered. "I can put it in the trunk or take it inside. What's your preference?"

"Put it in the trunk. Brandon's not selling anything yet."

And as soon as he was, Trish knew that Barb would be one of the first to purchase. She had said so at least three times already today. There wasn't a grandmother Trish had ever met who was prouder of her grandkids than Barb was.

"Ready?" Trish stood in front of Barb.

"As soon as you listen to me."

Trish closed her eyes and shook her head. She should know by now that what Barb wanted, Barb got. "Fine." She folded her arms across her chest. "But it won't change my mind about marrying anyone."

"Oh, I know, and I meant what I said about accepting your answer on that. Come closer and give me your hand."

"Barb, it's cold."

"Which is why you should give me your hand immediately. You wouldn't want to be the cause of an old lady freezing to death, now, would you?" The statement was said with a grin.

Trish stepped forward and held out her hand.

"It hasn't slipped my notice that you don't have any family around to care for you, or you didn't until your brother arrived. And you know that I know you have another brother and a sister. I don't know what's wrong with them, but I know they're absent." She squeezed Trish's hand firmly. "I'd like you to marry one of my grandsons because I'd really like to have you for a granddaughter. However, since you say that's not going to happen, I'm just going to adopt you right here and now. From this time forward, you're my granddaughter – honorary as it might be and less legal than if a lawyer or a marriage certificate was involved but no less true. There, now we can go in." She let go of Trish's hand and began walking toward the entrance to Brandon's studio.

Trish stood where she was as if rooted to her spot by the idea that Barb wanted her as a granddaughter. The thought was as heartwarming as it was startling. However, there was that past that no one knew about.

"You don't want me." Trish blinked against the tears that gathered as she finally followed Barb toward the door.

"I just said I did."

"But you don't know..." She looked down the alley. They were alone. "You don't know what I've done." The words were hard to push out, but she managed it.

"Whatever it is, it doesn't matter. I know the girl you are."

"No, you don't. You only know who you think I am."

Barb stopped about a metre from the entrance. "Then, before we go in, tell me why I can't love you."

Love? Trish blinked.

"You heard what I said. Go ahead and tell me before you turn blue and can't move and I have to drag you inside."

Oh, Barb was a demanding woman. Trish's heart raced. She knew that aside from going in without her or picking her up an carrying her, Barb was going to stand right where she was until she had heard what she wanted to hear.

Trish looked up and down the alley again. It was still as empty as it was before. Why couldn't a garbage or delivery truck or even a kid on a bike drive down the alley right now so she wouldn't have to make this confession.

"I won't tell a soul, my dear. Not a soul."

"Promise?" Trish twisted her hands together. She didn't want to have to leave Hatfield Falls. She liked it here. But if her past became known...

Barb nodded.

Trish looked down at her hands. "I was the other woman."

"Is that all?"

Trish's brow furrowed. "What do you mean is that all? I dated a married man while his wife was sick. I only discovered that he was married when I went to surprise him by visiting his church and the pastor's wife pulled me aside after she greeted me and told me that he wasn't there because his wife had died two days earlier." She rested her hands on her abdomen. The memory of that day always made her feel ill.

She had felt utterly humiliated to discover the truth after so proudly declaring Michael was her boyfriend when asked about how she knew him. She shook her head, trying to clear the images and voices that were there. To be honest, the pastor's wife had been very kind about the whole thing, and Trish could have slipped away to cry and puke in her car alone, without anyone else knowing what she was, had it not been for the lady in the red dress, wearing the obnoxious perfume, who had overheard the exchange, and who had been far less kind. She was the one who had used the information about Trish's name and where she lived and went to church to shame her. Trish's lips trembled.

"He duped you?"

She nodded. Tears began to fall.

"I don't know how to ask this gently, my dear, but how far did he seduce you?"

Trish sniffled and brushed at her tears with her gloved hand. "I went to see him to tell him I was pregnant. He hadn't answered any of my texts or calls." She should have known there was a reason for that, and that the true reason was not just that he was busy.

"And the child?" Sadness etched Barb's features and filled her eyes.

Trish shook her head.

"Did you have an abortion or give it up for adoption?" Barb's voice was soft and gentle. There was no condemnation or horror in her tone.

"I had a miscarriage," Trish whispered. The tears began falling in earnest now. How often, in solitude, had she cried over the loss of her baby? "I know I should be happy that I did not end up a single mom, but I can't be."

"Who told you that you should be happy about that?" Barb demanded as she moved to the door. Now, her tone had an edge to it, but Trish knew that Barb's anger was not directed at her. "It was a child. Plain and simple. Was it your parents who said that?"

Trish only nodded as she followed Gran into the studio because she did not trust herself to speak. It hadn't only been her parents though. The matter had been brought up before the church at an impromptu meeting during

Sunday School about a week after the miscarriage had happened. She had left as soon as she could extricate herself from the room and had never returned to church. That was why her parents had kicked her out on Christmas Eve two years ago. She had refused to attend church, and therefore, was no longer welcome in their home. Her mother had cried. Her father had glowered. It was impressed upon her that she should be ashamed. After all, they were ashamed and were certain that God would punish her even more than He had done already by taking the child's life and the life of Michael's wife.

"Gran?" Brandon stepped into the back room when the bell on the door rang. "What's wrong?" he asked when he saw Trish.

"Nothing you need to worry about," Barb said. "We were having some girl talk, and it got a trifle overwhelming. It might be a good idea if we let my new granddaughter have some time to collect herself while you show me what you have done with this place."

Trish looked at Barb in confusion. "You still want me?"

"Oh, you're going to have to work harder than that to change my mind, my dear."

Brandon looked between them. "I'm not sure what you two are talking about, but if I've learned anything dealing with my sister, mom, and Gran over the years, it's that, when it comes to girl talk, the little I know, the better."

Despite her tears, Trish laughed at that.

"Are you certain you want to be alone?" Brandon's expression was as serious as she had ever seen it. "I can call your brother if you need."

"No, I'll be okay. Barb's right. I just need some time." And a different past. Of course, a bit of time was a lot easier to find than a history that was washed clean of her sins was. "I'll join you soon."

"You're sure?"

Trish nodded.

"Ok, then. The bathroom in my apartment is in working order. The one down here still needs a sink."

"Thanks." She cast a worried look in Barb's direction, but it was met with a smile as Barb pretended to lock her lips.

Trish breathed a sigh of relief. Her secret was safe, or so it seemed. She placed a hand on her chest and let it rise and fall with her breaths. Strangely, something inside of her felt lighter.

"I adopted her," she could hear Gran saying out in the studio area. "Just now. In the alley."

"That's not how adoptions work," Brandon said.

"Do you want me to unadopt her?"

"No, no, that's not what I was saying." Trish could hear the frustration in Brandon's voice. "I'm fine with you having more grandchildren."

"You could get married and give me one more."

"Gran! I'm not ready to even think about marrying anyone."

"That woman who broke up with you is a fool."

"She's not a fool, Gran. We just weren't right for each other."

Trish had heard the story about Brandon's break up, and she had to agree with Barb. That woman had been a fool, but then, she hadn't been any brighter. She put her coat and gloves on a chair near one of the three workbenches and went upstairs to wash her face and blow her nose.

"She still wants you," she said to herself in the mirror. "She still wants you." She shook her head. It was almost too good to be true. Someone, who knew her shameful secret, was not going to turn up her nose at her or look at her with sad, but condemning, eyes. This family was so different.

Downstairs, the bell on the back door rang. Boots thumped up the stairs. One of the workmen must be back to continue whatever was being done up here. Brandon hoped to be moved out of Henry's place by the end of February when the studio opened.

She gave herself one more appraising look in the mirror, tossed her tissue in the garbage can, and walked out the door and straight into the guy who had come up the stairs but was not a workman.

"What are you doing here?" she asked Henry at the same time he asked her the same thing.

He held up a Drummonds bag. "Helping Brandon by bringing some supplies, and you?"

"Barb insisted on visiting the studio while she still could."

The man in front of her attempted a smile. It was a small peek at the soft heart that lay behind his boisterous exterior. That was one of the things that made her prefer him over his brothers or any other guy she had ever dated. There was more to him than met the eye. She had not seen it at first, but slowly, here and there, over time, she had caught glimpses of vulnerability beneath the bravado.

"She was being dramatic," Trish assured him. "She's going to be fine."

"Yeah, I know she will be, but..."

"The thought of it all is a little daunting."

Henry nodded. "And my faith might not be as strong as it should be." He moved toward the kitchen, and Trish followed. "Did you see the display Brandon was working on?"

"No, I just brought Gran in, and needed to blow my nose, so Brandon sent me up here. He said the sink is still not in downstairs."

Henry's brow furrowed. "They still haven't finished that? I thought it was supposed to have been done already." He shrugged. "I guess that's how renovations go. Sometimes, they are on time and other times, they aren't. Although with Nate..." His voice trailed off, and the furrow between his eyes, which had disappeared, returned.

"Even Nate can't guarantee things won't go wrong," she offered.

"Yeah, you're right. It just seems odd." He plopped the bags he carried on the counter. "I was specifically told to just put them in here and leave them. So, do you wanna go see that new display with me?"

"Sure."

He poked his elbow out, and she slipped her hand around it.

"Did Gran get all her errands done?"

"She did. Thanks for helping her with the coffeemaker. I know she had her heart set on that particular one. I'm glad you were able to order it from another store."

There was just enough room for them to walk down the stairs together if they stayed close.

"I'll have it set up for her before she goes to the hospital next week."

Trish heard the breath he expelled. It was one that was weighed down with worry. "She really will be fine."

"Are you reassuring me or yourself?" he asked.

"Maybe both of us." Barb was not young. Things happened during surgeries. And those two facts did concern Trish.

"Yeah? Do you care that much about all your library patrons?" his tone was light, teasing, and just what she needed. She wondered if he knew that. He seemed to have an uncanny ability to read her. It was what frightened her most about letting herself get close to him.

"Library patron? What a thing to call my grandmother!"

"Your what?"

"My grandmother."

He looked at her in question.

"She adopted me just now in the alley before we came in."

"She did?"

Trish nodded.

"Don't take this the wrong way, but did she say why she was adopting you in an alley?"

Trish chuckled. "Apparently, she likes me."

"That's easy enough to understand," Henry muttered.

"And since I wouldn't agree to her bargain of ginger snaps in exchange for marrying one of her grandsons, she decided to adopt me."

Henry laughed. "She was trying to sell us off for cookies?"

"Not just any cookies. Ginger snaps, which are slightly, and only slightly, higher in value than oatmeal raisin."

"I see. So, you can be bought off with baked goods?"

"It depends on the deal."

"Does that mean you're saying I'm worth more than a favourite cookie?" He smirked.

Trish shook her head. "If it helps you sleep at night, Bennett."

"It just might if you say Brandon is only worth an oatmeal raisin cookie."

She stopped walking and looked at him. His vulnerability was showing again. Was he jealous of his brother? That made no sense. "Why?" she asked, and the crack in his façade closed.

"Older brother, younger brother." He shrugged as if it was nothing more than that, which, of course, meant it was more.

"Say," he continued, "I was planning to come by the library tomorrow to find you, but since you're here, I'll ask now. I get together with a couple of friends before Sunday school each Sunday for breakfast at a diner. I was wondering if you and Trevor might like to join us. It'd be my treat for you guys just like it is for my friends."

"You pay for breakfast for your friends every Sunday?" That was generous.

He nodded. "It was the only way I could get them to come to church with me years ago," he said it as if it was an embarrassing confession, "and the tradition has kind of just stuck."

"Trevor and I are already going to go to your church on Sunday, so there's no need for a bribe."

"I know, but," he looked toward the studio door, "I'd like to get to know you... and your brother better."

Was there a reason why he had hesitated after saying *you*?

"And, it would give Trevor a chance to meet a couple more people."

Now, he was working the situation. She had had her fill of games guys played. "Do you really want me there or just my brother?"

His eyes held hers for five loud heartbeats before he spoke.

"Honestly, I'd be okay if your brother and my friends ditched, and it was just you."

"I'm not looking for a boyfriend." Even if the guy she wanted for a boyfriend was presenting himself as an option.

He nodded. "I kind of thought so." He looked down at the floor. "But, I can settle for friends."

She stepped closer to him. "It can never be more." She needed him to understand that. "Not for all the ginger snaps in the world, and I love ginger snaps."

Again, he nodded. "I know the risk. Will you come?"

"With my brother?"

"If necessary," he replied with a grin. "Seriously, I'd like to get to know him, too."

"Text me the details. We'll be there." It was probably stupid to agree to this, but then, she was familiar with making dumb choices when it came to men, wasn't she? Somehow, she doubted that saying yes to meeting Henry for breakfast was going to lead to destruction. That is, it wouldn't lead to destruction of anything more than what remained of her heart, she thought belatedly as he typed his phone number into her phone, and she put hers in his.

Chapter 8

As he climbed out of his car, Henry waved to Paul and pulled his collar up a bit higher. A gust of biting wind made the black and turquoise Falls Diner sign rattle as if it was shivering just like Henry was.

"Cold enough for you?" Paul Lally, a gentleman in his late fifties and owner of the diner, called as he threw another cup of rock salt on the sidewalk.

"Too cold," Henry replied.

Paul's laugh puffed out in front of him. "We've got some messy weather coming."

"So I've heard." Standing in front of the door to the diner, Henry clapped his hands together and gave them a rub. He should have worn his thicker gloves.

"I think we'll be closing early today. Probably after the lunch crowd clears out. No point in staying open once the roads get bad, and I'd like the staff to be home and safe before that."

"Sounds like a good plan." Henry rubbed his hands together again.

Paul nodded towards the door. "Get yourself inside. Pam's waiting for you. I hear you need the big booth this morning. Got more than the three of you coming, do you?"

"Yep. I've got a couple of new friends joining me today." Henry had called ahead to make sure the biggest booth in the small diner on the edge of town would be open. He waved to Trish and Trevor as they pulled into the parking lot.

"A girl, huh? Does your mom know?"

"She's just a friend." Even if he wanted her to be more than a friend, that was all Trish was.

"Who's the fella?" Although Paul had told Henry to go inside, he was making it challenging for Henry to do so.

"Her brother. He just moved to Hatfield Falls." Henry rubbed his hands together again. A toque would have also been good if he had known he'd be standing outside having a conversation. His ears were getting cold enough to sting.

"Do they need a church?"

Henry smiled. "No, they've already started attending church, which you would know if you could get a day away from here."

"I've got the radio on in the back, and as I told Pam, that'll have to do for now."

"Are you short staffed again?" It seemed a common problem for the diner. There was a core staff who had been here for years, but there always seemed to be someone starting or leaving. It wasn't uncommon for Paul to be short on wait staff or line cooks.

"Margot is off having a baby, so we are for a while."

"I'll keep my ears open and direct anyone to you if I hear of someone looking to wait on tables." He turned to Trish and Trevor. "Good morning."

"Good morning," Trish said with a smile. "You could have waited inside for us."

Paul laughed. "That's my fault, young lady. Henry here is too polite to cut a conversation short even when he's nearly frozen, and I'm too much of a talker." He dropped his cup in the salt bucket and stuck out his hand to Trish. "Paul Lally, owner of the diner."

"Trish Thompson," Trish said as she shook his hand.

"Trevor Thompson," her brother said when it was his turn to shake hands with Paul.

"Welcome to my place, and I really will let you get inside so my daughter can see that you're comfortable while you wait for the late brothers." He winked at Henry, who had opened the door and was holding it for Trish and Trevor.

"They aren't late yet," Henry replied, but if things went as they often did on Sundays, Blake and Tyler would arrive about ten minutes past the agreed upon meeting time, and Pam would have their coffee and pancakes waiting for them.

There were two older couples sitting in a booth about halfway down the line of turquoise and chrome tables that ran along the window. They smiled and one of the ladies gave a little wave as Henry passed on his way to the one corner booth in the place. These were the people he saw every Sunday morning. They would leave in about half an hour.

"How do you want to do this?" Trevor asked when they reached the large table at the end of the row of booths and with the bench that wrapped around the corner.

"I'm okay sitting between the two of you," Trish offered before Henry could suggest the same thing. "So, go ahead and slid into the corner, Trevor. I'll sit on this side with Henry, and Blake and Tyler can share the other side." She looked from her brother to Henry. "Will that work? They are capable of sitting beside each other, aren't they?"

"Yeah, they are most mornings."

"Coffee for everyone?" Pam said, coming up behind them with a tray of cups and a pot of coffee.

"Can I just have juice?" Trish asked.

"You don't drink coffee?" Henry asked.

"She already has," Trevor replied. "So have I, but I'd love another cup."

"What kind of juice would you like?" Pam asked as she placed four cups on the table and began to pour coffee into them. "We have tomato, apple, orange, and grapefruit." She placed saucers on top of two of the cups just as she always did to keep the coffee as warm as possible for Blake and Tyler.

Trish handed her jacket to Henry who hung it with his and Trevor's on the hooks on the wall at this end of the diner.

"Is it white grapefruit or pink?" Trish asked.

She was actually considering grapefruit juice? Henry hadn't met anyone younger than sixty who drank grape-fruit juice.

"Pink. Can I put you down for a glass of that?"

"A large one, please."

Apparently, though she was not sixty, she liked grape-fruit juice.

"I'll be right back with that for you." She looked at Henry who was just taking his place next to Trish. "Is everyone having the usual?" She slid a breakfast menu to Trish and Trevor.

"Yep, three stacks of pancakes."

"I'll let the cook know." She turned her attention to Trish. "You just take your time with that. There's no rush. Sunday school doesn't start for another hour and a half."

"She knows you're going to Sunday school after this?" Trish asked Henry when Pam had walked away.

"Pretty much everyone in here knows that. I've been eating here since I was in high school, although back in high school, I was not getting up early on Sunday mornings to eat breakfast here. Back then, Tyler, Blake, and I would roll through here on our way to have some fun on Friday or Saturday nights."

Trish cast a wary look at her brother. Hadn't she told her brother about his partying past? He had assumed she would.

"I used to do a lot of partying," Henry said to Trevor. "I'm not proud of it, but it is what it is. Let's just say that when I stopped coming in on Friday or Saturday night and started coming in early Sunday mornings, Pam and Paul took notice and wondered about the change." His ears burned with embarrassment. He had known he would have to explain his Sunday morning diner tradition, but even being prepared to do so didn't lessen the shame of actually doing it.

"And what a change it was," Pam said as she placed a large glass of pink juice in front of Trish. "It finally got Dad to visit church with me. He hadn't gone to church in years – ever since Mom walked out on him." She placed a hand on Henry's shoulder. "And Dad's not the only one who has taken note of the three guys praying over their food and having a good time on Sunday mornings." She reached into the pocket of her apron and pulled out an order pad. "Have you had time to decide?"

"I want the veggie omelet without onion," Trish said.

"Whole wheat toast?"

"Yes."

"And for you?" Pam asked Trevor.

"I'm a sucker for French toast."

"Do either of you want a side of bacon or sausage?"

"Sausage," Trevor replied.

"None for me, thanks." Trish said.

"I'll take her bacon," Blake said slipping into the booth about five minutes earlier than Henry had expected him to show up. "Hey, Trish."

"Extra bacon for Blake?" Pam asked Henry, who nodded. "And it's all together?" she asked softly as Trish introduced her brother to Tyler and Blake.

"Yeah, one bill."

"The food will be out soon," she said and left them.

"Trish mentioned you were really into the church thing," Trevor said.

Apparently, she had talked to her brother about him some. "I am, but as I was saying, it hasn't always been that way. I used to spend an incredible amount of time finding ways to avoid church, which, as you can imagine, isn't so easy when your dad's the pastor."

Trevor chuckled. "No, I suppose that does make it tricky. What did the church think of your way of living? I assume they must have known."

Ouch, that was a sore spot. "I didn't know it at the time, but Dad considered stepping down for a while. However, the deacons and elders wouldn't hear of it. They knew how my dad had tried to raise me and said that my sin was my sin and not his, and then, I became one of the permanent items of prayer during their weekly prayer time."

"That's all?" Trevor seemed startled by what Henry had said. "They didn't call you in or anything?"

Henry shook his head. "No, but they did their best to encourage me to attend youth meetings, and several of them made a point of stopping by Drummonds to say hi each week. They weren't going to let me forget that they were there for me – and my dad." He regretted the worry he had caused for his parents – his dad even more than his mom – and he now appreciated the love and grace that was shown to him when he didn't deserve it. Of course, at the time, he had only found it to be an annoyance.

"Huh." Trevor's eyebrows were lifted high. "That seems like the proper way to do things."

"It does," Trish whispered next to Henry.

Somehow, this information about how his church had responded to his sin seemed to touch on what had hurt her.

"I take it your former church wasn't like that?" he asked Trevor. Trish made a soft, snorting laugh sound as if he had asked some *bright* question like "so, dogs bark?"

"Not at all." Trevor's smile was tight, and Henry saw him slide his hand across the bench towards his sister. "That's why I'm here in Hatfield Falls. I had my fill of their lack of love and since Foster's Arm is so tiny, staying put wasn't going to work if I wanted to be free from them."

"Aw, man, that stinks!" Blake put Henry's mental response to Trevor's reply into words.

"Like the clean out under the sink," Trevor agreed before turning back to Henry. "So what flipped the switch for you?"

Henry waited until Pam had placed a plate of food in front of everyone. Then, after Tyler had thanked God for the food, he poured syrup on his pancakes and took a bite before replying with a single word. "Jake." It was just a name to most, but to him, that short, common-sounding name held a pile of guilt and shame that would dwarf Mount Everest.

"Who's Jake?" Trevor asked.

"He was a nerdy kid in school," Henry began the explanation he didn't want to make but he knew he had to. How was he supposed to help Trish if he covered his own painful memories?

"Scrawny little thing," Blake added.

"But with a brain the size of Saturn," Tyler said.

"And he was out in space a lot back when we were in grade eleven," Blake said.

"Jake came to Hatfield Falls High at the end of grade ten," Henry explained. "He was the kid everyone went to if they needed help with homework and also the kid whose name became synonymous with what not to be if you wanted to be cool."

"Until Henry befriended him." Tyler looked at Henry with caution in his eyes.

"Yeah," Henry said with a nod to Tyler to let him know that it was fine to discuss Jake. "He was a nice kid under the awkwardness, and he was hungry for friendship. Unfortunately, he was *blessed* with mine." He stuffed another bite of pancakes into his mouth to give himself an excuse not to speak for a minute.

"Jake kind of idolized Henry," Tyler explained. "He tried his best to be just like him."

And that was the problem. Jake had followed Henry into everything he could. Only, Jake tried to do it better or do more of whatever it was that he saw Henry do. It was as if he felt he had something to prove to everyone, and Henry supposed if he had been the object of jokes, he might have responded in the same way to cover what was laughable with something more popularly appealing.

"He died while boating the summer after we graduated. I wasn't here at the time, but I hear he and the others he was with were pretty drunk." Henry took a sip of his coffee. "I gave Jake his first beer. I took him to parties when he wasn't invited. I led him straight down the path to destruction just by being his friend." He put air quotes around the word friend.

"But he made his own choices." Trevor's words were spoken like someone who understood the pain Henry felt because of his own stupid choices.

"But would he have made them if I hadn't presented the choice to him?"

Trevor shrugged. "Maybe someone else might have given him worse choices. Maybe he would have made some all on his own."

"I suppose you might be right, but I feel responsible."

"That's understandable." Trevor's eyes flicked to his sister. "But you really don't have to carry the weight of it for life. I mean, I know there are lasting consequences, and the scars will never be erased, but we can be free from these things, can't we be?"

"Yeah, we can," Tyler inserted. "Many of us have done stupid things we regret."

"Not all of them have ended with someone dying," Henry countered.

"That's true," Tyler agreed.

Henry stabbed three pieces of pancake with his fork. "What I did can't be undone, but I can learn from it and move forward." He put the pancakes in his mouth.

"Need a refill?" Pam asked.

"Please." Blake held out his cup. He was the only one who took a refill.

"That's why you do this." Trish made a circular motion with her finger indicating the whole table. "Jake is why you do all the church things – like with Linda from your work."

"In a way," Henry admitted. "Like I said to you the other night, how can I not be really into the God thing when I've been forgiven for so much – for putting my dad through grief, for wasting years and money, and for leading Jake down a wrong path." He blew out a breath.

"No," she said with a shake of her head. "It's more than that, though I suppose that is where it started. You lead people to God by being their friend."

Henry's lips curled up on one side. "I guess I do. I hadn't really thought about it like that. I've always just thought I was being a light and repaying the grace and love shown to me by extending it to others."

"She's right," Blake said. "You led me to God by being the most annoyingly determined friend I could ever have. Even Tyler was ready to give up on me, but you weren't."

"I almost did give up when you threw that bottle at me and told me to never come back."

Trish's hand came to rest on Henry's arm as if she instinctively knew that the memory of that night was deeply painful one. "You did that?" she said to Blake.

"Yeah, I can be a bit of a jerk. Not as often now as back then, but I'm a work in progress." He shook his head. "Preacher Boy Bennett here had pointed out a sin that hit a little too close to the heart –"

"And was one I had been guilty of at one time as well," Henry added. "So, to Blake, it seemed like I was trying to make myself out to be better than him or was saying one thing when I did another."

"But he wasn't doing that thing anymore," Tyler inserted. He always tried to prop Henry up when they began talking about the past and regrets. Tyler truly had the gift of encouragement. "In fact, I don't think he did it more than a couple of times, not that it makes it any better."

"It was once." That was another regret he felt deeply because he'd never get to experience his first time with his wife. He had given that away to a girl he had met on a trip to Ontario.

"Yeah, well, once was enough to justify my reaction in my mind," Blake said. "The point is that you didn't give up on me." He shrugged. "And I'm grateful that you didn't."

"So am I," Tyler said.

The table fell into silence as they each finished eating the food in front of them. Then, their conversation turned to more normal things such as the weather and what was happening in their lives at work.

"You're a good man," Trish said to Henry later as he helped her with her coat. "I almost wish I was looking for a boyfriend." Her cheeks flushed, and Henry's heart leapt.

"I completely wish you were, but I'm just going to be thankful that you want to be my friend and will, maybe, stop avoiding me?"

She held his gaze. "You scare me." She lifted one shoulder and let it drop.

He scared her? Wow! That was not something he expected her to say. "Like I make you want to sleep with the lights on?"

She laughed. "No. It's just you and your love for God and the way you seem to know what I'm thinking." She blew out a breath.

Ah! He made it hard for her to hide. He knew that feeling. Knowing he was going to have to share about Jake today had terrified him. Brandon had been right when he said Henry needed to stop hiding. Whether he spoke about his past or not, it was there, and surely, even something as terrible as leading a friend down a path that led to his death could be used for good in the hands of God, couldn't it?

"Are you still willing to be friends?" Had he blown his chance already? He motioned toward the door to the diner where her brother was talking with Blake and Tyler.

"According to Blake, I'm not sure I have a choice." Her smile was teasing.

He chuckled. "Maybe not, but if I gave you the choice?" He sucked in a deep breath as he waited for her to answer and whispered a prayer that she would not send him away.

"Yeah, I'd like to still be friends even if you are unnerving in some ways."

He stopped at the cash register and pulled out his wallet.

"Thank you for breakfast," Trish said. "See you in church?"

"Save me a seat?" he replied as he swiped his card across the reader.

"I'll see what I can do, but no promises."

"You coming, Trish?" Trevor called to her from the door.

"I've got the keys, so he'd better hope I am."

Henry laughed as he followed her to the door of the diner.

"She seems sweet," Pam said before Henry could duck out of the diner.

"We're just friends."

"Yeah? Looks like more."

"She's told me in no uncertain terms that she is not looking for anything more than friendship."

Pam smiled broadly. "So what I'm hearing is 'Pam, please pray that she changes her mind.'"

Henry chuckled. "I wouldn't be offended if you did pray for that, but..." He sighed.

"There's more, huh?"

Henry nodded. He and Pam had known each other for years, and not just from the diner. She was only four years older than him and had lived in Hatfield Falls and attended his dad's church, when the diner didn't get in the way, all her life.

"Putting it on the prayer list," Pam assured him. "Both the changing her mind and whatever the more is."

"Thanks, but please, don't tell my mom or my brothers that I'm okay with that."

"And risk not getting your tip?" She scoffed. "I'm smarter than that. Tell your dad that he'll be preaching to the kitchen and counter customers again today."

"Will do." Henry pulled up his collar and pushed his way through the diner's door and out into the bitter wind of a stormy January day.

Chapter 9

"Gran wants to talk to you before she leaves today." Edmund peered over the front desk to where Trish sat on the floor behind it, attempting to get the printer used to print out due dates to accept the new roll of paper. "I can do that if you want."

"No, I'm not going to be beaten by a piece of machinery." Trish scowled at the printer. "Now, be a nice boy, and let me feed you this paper."

"I don't want any paper."

She glared at Edmund. "Not funny."

Eddie held up his hands in defense. "Just trying to lighten the mood."

"I know, but this dumb thing won't cooperate." And she had been feeling rather testy for half a week now, so the fact that the paper wouldn't feed into the machine was an obstacle she just couldn't face with a pleasant attitude.

"Let me do it?" There was a pleading tone to his request. "Gran wants to see you, so you'd be doing me a favour."

Trish had been avoiding Barb today. She looked at the printer. "Do you hear that? If you don't take the paper this time, I'm going to let Eddie take over." She folded the end of the paper, stuck it between the rollers, and pressed the button. The machine made a whirring noise, but the rollers didn't move. "Have it your way." She rose from the floor. "There was some paper stuck in it, but I think I pulled it all out. I can't see any more stuck in there." She handed the roll of paper to Edmund. "I hope I didn't break it."

Eddie smiled. "If you did, maybe we'll finally get one that works every time we use it instead of just when the printer stars are perfectly aligned."

Trish chuckled. "Printer stars?"

Eddie shrugged. "You laughed so it worked." He moved to join her behind the desk. "You've seemed rather down this week, and," he blew out a breath, "I need a bit more happiness around me today."

She nodded her head. "Yeah, I know the feeling, and she's not even my grandmother." Tomorrow was Barb's hip surgery.

"Shhh. Don't let her hear you say that."

"Well, I'm not her real granddaughter."

"Maybe not in your mind, but in hers, you are." He knelt next to the printer. "So try to remember to call her Gran." He gave her a stern look.

"But that feels weird."

"Just do it." He sat back on his heels. "Is it just Gran's surgery that has you out of sorts?"

"Maybe." It wasn't, but she was not about to discuss anything else with Edmund. He didn't need to know that she liked his brother far more than she was supposed to. Nor did he need to know that she had been wrestling with something she had heard in church on Sunday. These were best kept to herself. "I'll go see Barb. Gran," she corrected when Eddie arched one eyebrow over a displeased look.

"Take those magazines on the shelf over there to Lacey on your way, please."

Trish grabbed the stack of magazines that needed to be shelved and walked slowly toward the reading area that was next to the magazine racks. The thoughts that she had been avoiding while grumbling at the printer pushed their way forward. Could something good truly come out of her poor dating choices and the loss of a baby who had only just been known to her for a few weeks? It seemed impossible, but Henry had said that he was moving forward using what he had learned to the glory of God and the good of others. She smiled. He hadn't actually said those words. Those were the words his father had used in his sermon about Joseph on Sunday morning.

"Are those for me?" Lacey asked when Trish got to the reading area.

"Yep. I'd offer to help you put them away, but Eddie says Gran wants to see me."

Lacey clutched the stack of magazines to her chest as if hugging them could help soothe her soul. "She talked to me before my break."

Ah, that explained the fact that Lacey's eyes were slightly red.

"It's just hip replacement surgery," Lacey said. "But..."

"It's still surgery," Trish finished. She and Lacey had discussed Gran's surgery last week after Trish had spent the day shuttling Gran around for her errands.

"I'm just finding it hard to leave it in God's hands today," Lacey admitted. "I'll likely be even worse tomorrow.

But what can I do to protect her, or Will or Mrs. Bennett or Emma or any of the others if things don't go well?" She shook her head. "Nothing."

Trish blew out a breath. "Yeah, I know. It's hard to leave things with God sometimes." She took a step away from Lacey. "I'll let you get those back in place before our talking about Gran starts us both crying."

"Again," Lacey said with a nervous laugh.

Trish looked around the area. The library had been pretty empty today, and this area didn't have a single person in it at present, so she crossed over to Lacey and gave her a quick hug. "She's going to be fine." And if she said it enough, she might actually believe it. "God is good, right?"

Lacey smiled. "He is, even when other things aren't."

And that was the part that Trish struggled with the most.

The lights flashed on and off, signalling that closing time was quickly approaching.

"She'll be turning off her computer soon," Lacey cautioned.

"I'm going." Was every Bennett in the library going to make her feel like an errant child? She shook her head. No, that was her own doing. They were merely directing her to where she should have already taken herself.

"It's about time." Barb sat at her computer station with a black screen in front of her. "I was just about to come looking for you."

"I had work to do."

"This library could've had one librarian in it today, and there'd be time for him or her to do extras," Barb grumbled.

"Did you enjoy yourself?" Trish sat down next to Barb at the computer table.

"I did. I like coming here and seeing people. You know I do have one of these things at home." She motioned to the computer. "It's a cute little blue laptop. Brandon said he'll make sure that it is connected to the hospital Wi-Fi for me when I'm ready for it." She pulled out her phone. "And look at this." She tapped on the screen a couple of times and then turned it so that Trish could see what was there. "My coffee maker is set up, and see that nifty thing next to it?"

Trish leaned forward and looked closely at the picture of a coffee maker on the counter at Barb's apartment.

"Henry got me a special container for those pods and filled it up with things he thought I might like." She turned the screen back towards herself and smiled. "The mocha hot chocolate is to die for." She sighed. "I might ask him to replace all the other things with that." She laughed. "He's sweet enough that he'd do it, too."

Trish knew that it was true.

"You know, all his life he was the one grandchild who I knew would drop whatever he was doing to come help me with something. Even in his wild days, he took time for me." She tucked her phone into her purse. "The others were helpful and willing as well, but there was something special about Henry." She looked to her left and her right. "He has a good bit of his mom in him," she whispered it as if it was a secret. "Amy always reminded me of her father."

"And now, Henry reminds you of your husband?"

Barb nodded. "He does. Some girl," she gave Trish a pointed look, "is going to be very fortunate to marry him some day."

"I most heartily agree, but then, any girl who marries any of your grandsons is going to be fortunate."

"Yes, but I think you understand my meaning." She winked.

Oh, Trish had a crystal-clear picture of what Barb hoped would happen. "I can't," she said with a shake of her head.

"And I'm still praying. But, that's not what I wanted to talk to you about. I know that surgeries don't always go as planned by us. They always go as God plans them, but who are we to know the plans of God or understand His grand design." She rummaged around in her purse. "I wanted to make sure that each of my grandchildren had something from me, and I wanted to be the one to give it to them. Yours is the final gift. I've managed to see all the others."

"Gran, you don't have to."

"I didn't say I had to. I said I wanted to. The two are very different." She held out a box that was about the size of one of those oversized index cards. "A token of my love."

Trish lifted the lid off the box. Inside was a small note-book.

"I've written things in that book just for you."

Trish lifted startled eyes to Barb. "You wrote things in here for me?" She flipped through the notebook. Sure enough, the pages were covered in elegant handwriting. "This must have taken forever."

"I started it just after Thanksgiving. I didn't know you very well before that."

"You don't know me very well now."

Barb shook her head. "I know plenty about you. I might wear glasses, but I'm not blind."

"You've been watching me?"

"Yes, I have, and I've also been listening to Lacey and Brandon talk about you. They really enjoy your friendship, and they aren't alone. I'm happy for it, too. Oh, it might have started as you just putting up with a difficult old lady, but we both knew, even before I adopted you, that our relationship was more than that. Just as naturally as a tree sprouts from a seed and pushes its way up into the sky, I have grown to love you."

Tears sat barely contained in Trish's eyes. "Why? How?"

Barb shrugged. "I think God put you in my heart."

Trish shook her head. "I don't deserve this," she whispered.

"One doesn't ever deserve love," Barb said. "It's not something you earn. It's something that is given and hopefully, returned. However, sometimes it's not, and that's as painful as it's true." She took the notebook from Trish and flipped it open to the third page in. Then, she handed it back and tapped the page. "Read that please."

"Out loud?"

"No, not unless you want to."

From the look on Barb's face, Trish knew that her adopted grandmother wanted to hear her read what was written. So, she took a breath and read the familiar words.

"*For God so love the world that He gave His one and only Son, that whoever believes in Him shall not perish but have eternal life.* John 3:16."

"I'll let you read the rest of what I've written by yourself and whenever you want to do it, but I could not leave here today without sharing God's love with you. He offers it freely. Have you ever accepted His gift of His Son?"

Trish nodded and brushed at her tears. "When I was eight." And no one in her old church had ever cared enough to double check on that fact. Not all of them knew how she had raised her hand in children's church and been helped to pray to God, asking Him to forgive her of her sins.

Barb pulled a pack of tissues out of her oversized purse. "Good," she said as handed the tissues to Trish. "Then, I know that whatever happens tomorrow, I will see you again, and," she lowered her voice, "we'll both get to meet that little baby you lost."

She most certainly did not deserve this. "You..." she started. "I..." This woman who knew so little about her wanted to meet a child that had been conceived through a relationship that was not God-honouring? It really was too much for her to comprehend.

"I love you no matter what you did or do. All you have to do is accept my love and maybe return it when you can."

Trish threw her arms around Gran and squeezed her close. Had she ever known love that was this unconditional in her life? Sure, her brother seemed to love her despite her past, but he was her brother. Barb was basically a stranger who had simply chosen to love her.

"My sweet girl," Barb said softly as she returned Trish's hug. "You are to know everything that is happening with me while I am in the hospital, and I expect you to visit me. I'll be back here as soon as they allow me to be, but it could take a while. I'm not young, and we don't know how my body will heal."

"I'll visit. I'll do whatever you need me to do." Trish released her hold on Barb. How could she not willingly do whatever was needed after being given such a wonderful gift as Barb's love?

"There's Henry..."

"Except marry a grandson."

Barb smiled. "It was worth a try."

"I suppose it was." Trish dried her eyes and blew her nose.

"Are you making her cry again?"

Trish turned to find Brandon walking towards them.

"It seems I am," Barb backed her chair up and turned toward the aisle. "I think she just needs more people to tell her that they love her." She winked at Trish. "You know, to toughen her up to such things."

"Gran," Brandon said. There was a note of warning in the word.

"Oh, I'm not even trying to suggest that she should marry you."

"Why?" Brandon asked in surprise.

"Do you want me to suggest that?" Gran asked.

"No, but I'm curious about why you aren't, because that's rather unlike you."

"She's not your type." Gran gave Trish another wink before wheeling her way toward the door to the computer room.

"What does that mean?"

"It means you wouldn't suit." She paused at the door and waved to Trish before asking Brandon, "Did Henry come with you?" while locking eyes with Trish.

"She knows I'm not going to marry anyone," Trish called after them.

Barb shrugged, and Trish could almost hear the thought that accompanied the gesture. She shook her head and looked down at the notebook in her hand. Not even God could rid her of her past. No matter how much Barb prayed that Trish would marry Henry, it wasn't going to happen. Her past was there. It was always going to be there, standing between her and happiness. Or, at least, it was standing between her and a married kind of happiness. However, there might be a sort of happiness that could come from her past if she could just figure out how God could use her experience for good.

"Hey, Gran said you were in here."

Trish stopped paging through her notebook and looked up to find that Henry had come with Brandon.

"We're taking Gran over to Mom's for dinner tonight. Do you want to come?" he asked.

She shook her head. "Thanks, but I'll eat with Trevor."

"Okay, if that's what you want." He didn't move from where he was. "Brandon said Gran made you cry."

Trish held up the notebook Barb had given her. "She gave me a sweet gift and said she loved me." She shrugged. "It was a bit overwhelming, I guess." That was an understatement.

Henry pulled out a chair and sat down.

"Isn't Gran waiting?" Trish asked.

"Yeah, but I want to make sure you're fine."

"I'm good. Truly."

"You're sure?"

Trish nodded. "I know it seems silly that a little gift and being told you are loved would be overwhelming, but those are not normal parts of my life."

"They should be," he said.

She knew he was right. "Whether that is true or not, they just haven't been." She opened the book to the page Barb had made her read. "She wrote all these things here just for me, and she made me read this one." She handed the book to Henry. "Then, she asked me if I had ever accepted Christ. It seems you are more like your grandmother than I thought." Salvation was one of the first Bible-related things Henry had ever talked to her about.

Henry smiled as he read the words on that page. "She has never been shy about her love for God." He looked up at Trish. "And she did not hold back on pointing out my sins when I was in high school. I don't know how many times she asked me that same question, and it was always followed by a 'make sure you are so that I can see you in heaven.'"

That sounded familiar. "She said something like that to me as well."

"She's a pretty amazing lady."

"She is."

"Are you working tomorrow?" Henry asked as he handed the notebook back to Trish.

"I am. Are you?"

He nodded. "I have some paperwork to do tomorrow morning. Can I text you during the day? Just to check up on how you're dealing with things, and so you can remind me that she's going to be okay?" He stood, and so did Trish.

"I'd like that. I'll have Lacey here, but I'd still like that. You'll need someone." She followed him out of the room and towards the entrance.

"Fred's working, but I doubt he'd appreciate me sticking my head under the hood of a car and asking him how he was doing or if he thought Gran was out of surgery yet."

Trish laughed. "I bet everyone else at the store would find that entertaining."

"Probably, but I'd rather not be the store entertainment." He stopped just before he got to the front desk. "Any chance you'd want to hang out with a friend tomorrow night? I'm in charge of cooking, so we're having pizza and watching TV. Trevor's welcome to join us, too."

That seemed a little too close to a date. "I don't know." If it had been Brandon who had asked her, maybe she would have answered differently, but Brandon asking her to do something with him didn't cause her stomach to do that fluttery thing like it did when Henry was the one asking.

He just looked at her for a moment before saying, "No problem. Maybe another time?"

"Maybe."

He gave her a half-smile and a nod before walking away.

Oh, how she wished things could be different than they were. She took out her phone and typed, *Just testing to make sure the number still works before tomorrow.* Then, she watched as he read the text and turned to give her a full-smile and a thumbs up.

Chapter 10

"Hey." Fred dropped into the chair next to Henry's desk in his office at Drummonds. "Have you heard anything yet?" He pulled open the wrapper of his granola bar.

"Nope. This morning, Mom said she'd call as soon as she knew Gran was out of surgery and in recovery." He glanced at the clock. How long did hip replacement surgery take? Her surgery was supposed to start at eight this morning, and it was already quarter to eleven.

"She told me the same thing yesterday. I just thought she would've called by now." Fred took a bite of his snack just as Henry's phone buzzed.

"Is it Mom?" he asked around his mouthful of nuts, oats, and dried fruit.

"No, It's Trish."

"Has she heard anything?" he asked between chews and just before he swallowed.

"She says Will just called Lacey, but she doesn't know what he said because Lacey walked off to talk to him." Henry's phone buzzed again. "She says she doesn't see tears so she's going with things are fine." The message was punctuated with several silly emoji faces that caused Henry to smile.

Fred held up his phone. "Eddie said he just got a thumbs up from Lacey and a smile."

"Yeah, I just got a thumbs up, too."

Fred put the remaining two-thirds of his granola bar on Henry's desk and typed a reply to Eddie. "Do you like her?" He asked as he tapped his screen.

"What?"

"Do you like Trish? It seems like you do, but neither Eddie nor I can tell for sure, and Brandon refuses to speculate."

"Yeah, I like her." There was no reason to deny it. Something told him that being caught lying about anything that had to do with Trish was something that would push her further away – even if it was something as normal as denying to your brother than you liked a girl to avoid teasing. "But that's as far as it goes. She's not looking for a boyfriend. So, we're just friends."

"That's rough." Fred picked up his granola bar again. "Maybe she'll change her mind."

"Maybe." Henry leaned back in his chair. "Are you still admiring Melissa from afar?" Melissa was a cute blonde who worked in the clothing store that was next to Drummonds. The place where Fred bought nearly all of his work clothes.

"Nah, I actually went to lunch with her the other day."

"Really?"

Fred nodded.

"Trish says that Lacey says Gran is sleeping, and the surgery went well," Henry read from his phone just as it began to chime with his mother's ringtone. "Can you hold on just a minute, Mom?" Henry asked when he answered. Then, he pressed his phone to his chest. "Was the lunch good or bad?" he whispered.

"She's prettier when you look at her than when you talk to her," Fred replied.

"Sorry, Mom. Fred's here so I'll put you on speaker and then, you don't have to make as many calls."

"Thanks, sweetie. I wanted to call you sooner, but the nurse came in to check on things. Gran is still sleeping and hooked up to all kinds of machines."

The steady, rhythmic beeping of a heart monitor in the background was oddly reassuring to Henry. It was almost as if Gran were there, telling him she was doing fine.

"The doctor said he hasn't had a surgery go so smoothly in his career," his mom continued, "so he doesn't expect any complications. However, that doesn't mean he isn't prepared for some, nor is he giving us the all-clear just yet. He seems to be a very cautious sort of guy."

"Better that than too carefree," Fred said.

"Oh, I agree, and so does your father. We are very impressed by him. Dad has invited him to church, of course, so you might get to meet him if he ever does show up."

"I'm surprised that Gran hasn't had him there already," Fred said.

The three of them laughed at that.

"Actually, he did tell your father that Gran has invited him to church to meet her family twice already."

That was Gran. She wasn't afraid to invite people into her life or her church. She had a large group of acquaintances and a slightly smaller circle of friends. However, her intimate circle of cherished people was reserved for those dearest to her heart – her best friends of many years, her family, and Trish.

"I really don't know more than that," his mom said. Henry looked at Fred in confusion. Had he missed something important?

"Brandon is going to set up her laptop for her tonight because she has to stay a couple of days," Fred said.

"What?" their mom asked.

"Henry wasn't paying attention," Fred explained.

"Sorry," Henry said. "I was thinking about Gran and how welcoming she is."

"She always has been," their mom said. "Speaking of that, I asked Brandon if he'd call Trish and fill her in on Gran, but he said I should ask you to do it, Henry."

"He did know," Fred muttered with a shake of his head. "I knew he knew."

"What did Brandon know, honey?"

"That I like Trish," Henry answered.

"You do?" There was a note of caution in his mom's voice. That was odd.

"I do."

"And Brandon is okay with that?"

Ah, now the caution made sense. "Yeah, I think so. Not that it matters. Trish is single and wishes to remain that way."

His mom replied to that with a sad, drawn out "oh."

"Well, my break is nearly over so I need to head back to the garage," Fred said. "Thanks for letting us know about Gran, Mom."

"I'll call or text if anything changes," their mom assured him. Then, the call went silent until the door clicked behind Fred. "So, tell me about Trish," his mom said as is she had been waiting for Fred to leave, which was likely what she had done. "Does she know you like her?"

Henry rubbed his forehead with his right hand. "Yes, she knows."

"And she'd rather be single than date you?" His mother sounded absolutely astounded by the thought.

"Apparently, since I'm not dating her." And she hadn't even been willing to accept his offer to hang out as friends tonight when he had made it yesterday.

"I'm sorry, sweetie."

"I'm okay with it, Mom." Mostly.

"Henry." She drew his name out as if he were doing something he shouldn't be doing like she had when he was a kid.

"What other choice do I have?" None. Pressing the issue was not going to gain him ground where Trish was concerned. "Do you remember how I felt about Tyler and Blake after I got things right with God?"

"I do. Do you feel God's calling you to minister to Trish?"

Henry sighed. "Yeah, and that has to come first."

"Well, if that is how things are, I won't do anything more than pray for her and you. And I mean it. I've learned my lesson after what happened with Will."

"Thanks, Mom."

"I'd still like to see you get the desire of your heart though," she admitted.

"My desire is for her to be restored in her relationship with God."

"This isn't Sunday school, so don't give me the expected answer, Henry."

He smiled at her scolding tone. "I know, Mom, but it's true. That's my first desire." His other desires needed to be second to that.

"Then, I amend my statement. I'd still like to see you get *all* the desires of your heart."

Henry chuckled. "Me, too, Mom. Me, too." He sat forward. "So just keep praying."

"Oh, you know you can count on me to do that," she said with a laugh.

Henry knew it was true. His mom spent an hour each morning with her Bible and her prayer notebook sitting in her favourite chair in the living room, praying through scripture and for the needs of others. He had thought it was ridiculous when he was in high school, but now, he cherished her faithfulness to prayer, especially since he knew that on those mornings, when he was thinking she was being ridiculous, she had been praying for him.

"I love you, Mom."

"I love you, too, Henry. Just like I told Freddie, I'll let you know when Gran is awake."

"Let me know how soon she can have visitors."

"I will."

After his phone played the call ended tone, Henry opened his contacts and selected Trish's name.

Mom called. You were right. Gran's fine. At least for now, he thought as he sent the text.

Oooh, say it again, Bennett. Trish replied.

Say what?

That I'm right. The message was followed by three teary-eyed laughing faces and a second message. *Never been happier to be right. I was worried I would be wrong, and God would take her from us.*

Me, too, actually. Henry looked at the words. Did they say his faith was lacking? Probably. Was it okay to admit that he wanted to trust God but sometimes found it hard? He hit send. Whether it was okay to do or not, he was doing it. Trish had appreciated his realness on New Year's Eve. He doubted she would condemn him for admitting to having faith that still needed reassurance at times.

*Yeah? You were worried I'd be wrong? *smiley face**

She had just the right sense of humour to help him smile on a difficult day. *The God part.*

I know.

Still saying no to pizza tonight? It couldn't hurt to be persistent, could it?

Sorry but yeah.

Maybe persistence did hurt a little.

Mom's going to let me know when I can go see Gran. I'll let you know when she does.

Thanks.

The inventory forms on Henry's desk stared back at him when he set his phone aside. Maybe now that he knew Gran was doing well, he'd be better able to focus on them. Orders needed to be placed.

Two hours later, the work that needed to be done for the day was complete, and Henry tidied up his desk so he could head home. Picking up his phone, he typed, *Stopping at Friendly's on the way home. Anyone need anything?* into the message group he had set up for his brothers who lived with him.

No. I'm good. Eddie's answer popped up first.

Some of the good creamer, Fred's message came through on the heels of Eddie's.

Going to need extra pizza stuff. Brandon's reply was slower in coming. It had been slow enough that Henry had been able to get all his stuff put away and was just going to put on his jacket and head out.

Why? Henry asked.

Trevor was here working on the bathroom. It's all set by the way.

How does the mean more pizza stuff?

Oh, right! I asked him if he and Trish wanted to join us for supper. He said yes.

Another message popped up on Henry's screen.

Did you put him up to this, Bennett?

Henry sighed and dialed Trish's number. "No," he said when she answered. "I'm assuming you mean Brandon asking Trevor to come over to our place tonight. I just found out about it. Like one second before your text showed up." He slipped one arm into his jacket. Then, transferred the phone to his other hand so he could put his other arm into its sleeve. "Brandon doesn't even know I asked you."

"Are you telling me the truth?"

"I would never tell you anything but the truth, Trish."

"Never?"

"Never. Are you going to come over with Trevor or are you going to sit at home alone?"

"I'm used to sitting at home alone."

"I know you are, but is that what you're choosing tonight? Do want to avoid me that badly?" He stood with one hand on the door handle ready to open the door and leave his office. There was a long pause on Trish's end, and Henry braced himself for her reply.

"If you weren't a ginger snap." There was a note of what sounded like pain or regret in her voice.

She wasn't coming. Disappointment stabbed Henry's heart. It didn't matter that she had refused his offer yesterday. It still stung. Persistence could go take a nap. He didn't need or want it at present. "In that case," he said, "I hope you have a good night. I'll send some pizza home with Trevor."

"No," she said quickly before he could end the call. "No, it's not that I'm trying to avoid you." She sighed. "That's not true. I am trying to avoid you."

Wow. That hurt more than the disappointment a moment ago.

"Let me get away from where your brother can hear me."

Henry pulled open the office door and started walking down the hallway as quickly as he could. He'd rather not be at work when trying to process that sort of information. At least, his office was not far from the back door.

"You still there?" she asked.

"Yep."

"I don't want to avoid you. I just think I need to."

That wasn't helping him feel any better about the situation. "Do whatever you have to do, Trish." As if she was going to do anything other than that.

"I can't date you." Her voice was pleading. "I just can't. I wish I could. I wish it more than anything."

Henry stood at the back door. Snow flurries were falling again. The windshield of his car was covered with a light layer of snow. "Why can't you?"

"I... I... I just can't. It's not just you. I can't date anyone."

He pushed open the door and headed towards his car while holding the phone to his ear and not saying a word.

"Are you still there?" she asked.

"Yeah, I just don't know what to say."

"Say you understand?"

Frustration overwhelmed him. Should he just pretend to understand so that she would feel comfortable around him enough for him to talk to her about God? Or did he boldly step into what could be a rather messy and potentially fatal-to-any-relationship-possibility situation?

"But I don't, Trish," he said, choosing the latter option because it was the most real and honest. "I don't understand, and I'd like to." He opened the door to his car and, climbing in, he put his phone on the dashboard and hit speaker. "Here's the thing. I like you. A lot. And yeah, I'd like to date you. You know this. I told you as much at Brandon's studio. I also told you then that I'm willing to just be your friend. But I'm not going to force you to do what you don't want to do, and since friends hang out with each other and hanging out makes you want to hide from me, then maybe being friends is too much for us to be." There, he had put all his cards on the table. The next move was hers because he certainly wasn't going to make it unless God forced him to.

"Are you breaking up with me? Like we can't be friends anymore?"

Henry turned on the car and cranked up the defrost before flipping on the wipers to clear the snow from his windshield. "I'm trying to give you what you need. Work with me here. I like you. I'm willing to not date you and to just be friends, which, by the way, is not an easy choice. However, you're not really willing to even be that. What am I supposed to do? I don't want to give up on this. I promised God I would help you with whatever it is that keeps you away from Him. I don't want to give up on you."

There was no reply for a full minute.

"I'll be there tonight. You're right. I'm being silly. Friends hang out with each other, and I do want to be friends. I think I can do that."

"Hey, I don't want you to do this just because you think I'm giving you some sort of ultimatum. I'm willing to meet you wherever on this. If acquaintances who text each other and occasionally sit together in church is all you feel comfortable with, then, that's what I'll do. I won't be run off too easily, Trish." Even if it meant enduring a substantial amount of pain in the process. "Just ask Blake," he added.

"I don't have to ask him." Her voice was soft and not just in tone. "I trust you."

"Do you really?" Henry knew that, for her, trust did not seem to be given easily, and he needed to know that she was not just putting him off, that it was not just some sort of ploy to avoid him or something.

"Yeah, I do even though it scares me to do so." There was a short pause. "People I've thought I could trust in the past have turned out to be far from trustworthy."

"A boyfriend?"

"Yeah, and others."

"Your parents?" He heard her sigh and knew the answer was yes before she said it. "I'm not perfect, Trish, but I promise to do my best to be as trustworthy as any human can be. I know how precious trust can be and how difficult it is to reclaim once it's broken."

"Your parents?" she repeated his question back to him.

"Yeah. I seriously broke their trust. After I confessed to them all the stuff I had done behind their back – and in front of their faces – it took a full year before they relaxed and started believing that what I told them I was going to do was really what I was going to do." Oh, how he regretted having caused them so much pain.

"You told them everything?"

"Almost everything." There was that night in the boathouse at the lake that he hadn't shared.

"What did you hold back?"

Henry blew out a breath. Should he tell Trish about that?

"You don't have to tell me. Some secrets can't be shared. I get it."

That made his decision for him. Trust was a two-way street, and he had to walk down his part. "No one but Gran, Tyler, and Blake know about this."

"Gran? You told your best friends and Gran? How... Why?"

"Yeah, I know. It seems odd, but she's surprisingly good at getting me to share everything, and, when it comes to secrets, she's a vault with an impenetrable lock."

"She is. That makes sense."

Did Gran know Trish's secret? That was interesting.

"Oh, I don't want to share this," he said honestly.

"You don't have to."

"Yes, I do."

"Why?"

"Because you trust me, and I trust you. Okay, here it is. There was a girl I met in Ontario during my summer trip. One night there was a party on the beach. She was tipsy. I was more than tipsy. The boathouse was empty, and, well... we... we slept together."

"You're not a virgin?" Even though Trish was whispering, her surprise came through loud and clear.

"Nope, I'm not. I wish I were, but I'm not."

"Did she get pregnant?"

That was her question about this? Not did he love her? Or did he sleep with her more than once? Or what was her name? Or was she the only one? He tucked the oddness of the question into the back of his mind and answered, "No. The last I heard, she got back together with the guy who had dumped her that summer, and they're married now. No kids."

"Wow. You weren't kidding about being honest with me, were you?"

"I wouldn't joke about that."

"Yeah, I guess not."

"So, you're coming tonight? Because you want to?"

"Yeah, because I want to."

"I'm glad."

"Me, too."

"Is Hawaiian your favourite pizza? I'm stopping at the store on the way home to get supplies, so if it is, I'll grab some back bacon and pineapple."

"It's second to veggie pizza."

"Veggie pizza?" That was better than Hawaiian in his mind. "I can do that."

"No onions," she inserted quickly.

Another thing to remember about her. She disliked onions – at least, she didn't like them on pizza. "So peppers, mushroom, tomatoes, what else?"

"Black olives?"

"Sure. Anything else?"

"No. That's it. Can I bring some chips or something?"

"Just yourself, please."

"I can do that. I think. I'm not good at having friends. I used to be, but it's been a couple of years."

Henry put his phone on his thigh, tucking it under the edge of his jacket to hold it in place. Then, he put the car in drive. "You seem to do just fine being friends with Lacey."

"But she's Lacey," Trish protested.

"You've even been over to my place with her," he continued, "and you've been there with Brandon, too, whom you also seem to be able to be friends with without a problem." And, honestly, he was still jealous about that.

"Yeah, but remember, he's only maybe oatmeal raisin."

"Right. And I'm a ginger snap."

"Exactly."

"Are we friends or acquaintances?" He needed to know how to proceed because, at present, it felt like friends who were flirting, and that was a long way from acquaintances in his mind.

"Friends. I think I know too much to be just an acquaintance."

"As long as you're comfortable with it."

"I'm not, but I'm much less comfortable with not being friends. I'm sorry I can't be better at this."

"It's fine, Trish." It had to be. It didn't matter so much what he wanted right now. It was more about what she needed.

"No, it's not fine." She blew out a breath. "But it is what it is for now."

"It will get easier. You'll see. I'm actually not that bad of a guy. However, I should probably focus on driving," he added as a guy behind him honked. It was probably because he was still sitting at the stop sign when the road was clear. "I'll see you tonight?"

"I'll be there."

Henry tossed his phone on the passenger seat and as he pulled into traffic. He mentally listed the things to get at the store: pizza stuff, creamer for Fred, all dressed chips, one of those fizzy water things Trish liked, and, he smiled and nodded, ginger snaps. He was definitely going to get some ginger snaps.

Chapter 11

Friends. Trish blew softly through her lips. She could do this. Henry was just her friend.

Trevor poked his head back into his van. "You coming in or staying out here all night?"

"It's freezing. Why would I stay out here in the cold?"

Her brother shrugged. "I don't know, but you're sure taking your time getting out of the van, and you're right. It's cold out here." The snow squeaked under his feet as he did a little keep warm jig next to the open van door.

"I'm just a bit tired from work," she lied. She was tired, but that was not what was making her hesitate in getting out of the van.

"Yeah, like keeping books from losing their places is hard," he taunted. "If you'd rather, I could have you help me remove toilets and clean out traps."

"I'll have you know that I had a computer room full of teenagers today for the afterschool program, and I had to keep them from damaging anything or each other."

"Okay, you win. I'll take clogged sewer lines over teenagers any day. Just get out already."

"I am. See. Open door. Foot outside of it. You're so cranky when you're cold."

"And hungry," he added before giving his door a firm shove closed. "Brandon swears his brother makes the best pizza. Apparently, it's one of only a few recipes he knows how to cook well."

Trish laughed. "Pizza is kind of hard to ruin."

"Remember how Kayleigh always burns it?"

She smiled. "Kayleigh burns everything." She missed her little sister – even her inability to remember what she was supposed to be doing when cooking. "Do you think I'll ever get to have one of her blackened masterpieces again?"

Trevor put his arm around her shoulders. "I'll let her cook at my place once she's old enough to visit without parental supervision."

The last part of what he had said made her bristle. "You know Emma is nineteen, well, almost twenty, and she's started a business. I think that at twenty-one Kayleigh is old enough to visit her brother without Mom or Dad driving her and watching her every move."

"And you know what they would say to that, right?"

Oh, she knew. "Yeah, I'd get to be the object lesson of what happens when young ladies are not properly supervised."

"They'd say the same thing to Kevin if he was a year or two younger. In fact, I've heard them say it."

"Yeah? They pulled out the sinful older sister thing as a reason for him not to do something?"

"Yes, and no. It was a look at what happened with Trish, and then, they added, 'and your brother is headed the same way. This is what happens when children are given too much freedom.'" He shook his head. "I still can't believe they listened to rumours about me rather than listening to me."

"Well, the source of the rumours was the pastor's wife, so…"

"Yeah, I know. One must not question the pastor or his wife." His voice dripped with bitterness. "I'm glad the Bennetts don't seem like that sort of pastoral couple." He lifted his gloved hand and knocked on the door.

"Come in!" someone shouted from inside.

"They're really not. They're very different," Trish said as her brother pushed open the door to Henry's house. They were what she would want as a pastor and his wife, or… parents. She sighed. How she longed to just be wrapped in acceptance and love by her family – all of them.

"Their kids seem nice, too."

"They are." Trish began taking off her scarf.

"I think one of them likes you," Trevor said in a whisper.

"Do you?" Her cheeks grew warm. It was a good thing they were already rosy from the cold outside.

"Yeah, I'm pretty sure of it." Her brother hung up his coat and then gave her a questioning look. "I think you should consider him." He took her coat from her.

"I can't," she whispered. "And you know why."

Trevor slipped off his boots and put them on the boot tray under the coat hooks. "I think you're judging him too harshly. Not everyone is going to react to what you did the same way the people back home did."

"It doesn't matter how they react. I can't."

Her brother looked like he was about to launch into an older brother speech of some sort, but he didn't get the chance to.

"You made it." Brandon stood at the top of the stairs that led to the main level of Henry's split entry house. "Fred has movie choices to vote on, and Henry is just starting to assemble the pizzas. Come on up and make yourself at home. Not that I don't already know that Trish will." There was a hint of a question in his eyes.

Did he know that she was not thrilled to be here? Well, she'd prove to him that he was mistaken, even if he wasn't.

"Do you want something to drink?" she asked her brother. "Brandon here would be happy to get it for you."

Brandon laughed. "Yep, just like normal."

"You mean I'm not the only one she bosses around?" Trevor teased.

"Nope. Pretty sure all of my brothers get told what to do by Trish now and then. All in good fun, of course," he hastened to add before he stepped to the side to let them move past him into the living room. "I take that back. I don't know if I have ever heard her tell Henry what to do."

"Sure I have."

Brandon shrugged. "Maybe, but I'm having trouble remembering it."

"Interesting," Trevor hissed near her ear.

She jabbed him in his ribs and said, "They say the mind is the first thing to go when you get old."

Brandon chuckled. "Fine, we'll go with I'm old and not the 'you're interested in my brother' explanation."

"Shut up." She thwacked Brandon's arm. "I'm not..." She did not complete what she was going to say, since it would have been a lie. Henry interested her. A lot.

"Pick a good movie. I'm going to go make sure my pizza is done correctly." From the smirks her brother and Brandon both wore, that was probably not the thing to say or do, but it was too late now. She had only wanted to get away from her tormentors before she had to admit something she did not want to admit.

"I'm just about to do your pizza," Henry said as she entered the dining room, which was just on the other side of the kitchen island. "Want to help me?"

She looked at the bowls piled in the sink. "Did you make the crust?"

"Yep, and it's the best you'll ever have." He shot her one of his charming smiles. His over-the-top confidence about his pizza crust reminded her of their first official meeting at the orchard when he had struck a pose as if he was a model. The man was not shy about what he thought were his strengths.

"But did you make the sauce?" She asked as she went to the sink to wash her hands.

"Sort of."

"How do you sort of make pizza sauce?"

"You start with a can from the store and then add things to it." He grabbed a wooden spoon from the drawer next to the sink and, after dipping it in the sauce, offered it to her. "Best you've ever had."

She took the spoon and tasted the sauce. "Not bad."

"Not bad?" He huffed. "The can of sauce I started with was not bad."

She placed the wooden spoon in one of the bowls piled in the sink. "You can't judge a pizza sauce on its own. It has to be able to stand up to the crust and topping and tie them together exquisitely."

He cocked an eyebrow and gave her a doubtful look.

"Seriously. The sauce is good, and I can imagine it's fantastic on pizza. However, I'll wait to write my review until I have tasted the whole masterpiece." She grinned at him playfully.

He laughed. "I'll look forward to reading it." He passed her a bowl of sliced green peppers. "I'm glad you came."

"I am, too." Or she thought she was. She cast a look towards the living room. "Brandon seems to think I like you."

"You do, but it's only as a friend because anything else is too frightening."

He had her there.

"Does he know you like me?"

Henry nodded. "Yep, and I suspect so do Fred and Eddie since I told Fred I did."

Panic swelled inside her chest. "Why did you do that?"

"Fred asked me. Was I supposed to lie to him?"

She scowled. "No, I suppose not."

"I also told him that we're just friends."

"And he believed it?"

"He didn't tease me. Unlike Brandon." He rolled his eyes. "Olives." He handed her a second bowl. "I'll start getting these in the oven, and then, I can clean up while they bake." He picked up a meat-laden pizza. "Oh, put olives on the sausage pizza, please."

She did as he requested.

"I still see peppers in that bowl." He picked up a second pizza. That one looked like it was only pepperoni.

"My pizza didn't need them all."

He looked at the pizzas in his hands and the one non-veggie one on the counter. "Put them on the sausage pizza. Brandon likes olives and peppers. Sausage is his favourite."

"What kind is your favourite?"

"Anything but Hawaiian," he said with a laugh. "Of the four here, this one." He lifted the meat pizza he held. "Bacon, hamburger, pepperoni, sausage, and mushrooms. Hey, bring those over, and we'll get them all in."

She had noticed the top-of-the-line appliances in his kitchen the first time she had visited with Lacey. Okay, maybe they weren't top-of-the-line. There were probably more expensive ones to be had, but these were nice. And it was the first kitchen she had been in that had double ovens. Now she understood why he wanted that.

As she stood waiting for him to take the pizzas she held from her, she spotted a package of cookies on the counter. Were they? She took a step in their direction. They were!

"You bought ginger snaps?"

He grinned. "I did." He took her pizzas. "Just for you, although I'd love it if you'd share a few with me and, maybe, the others. I got ice cream, too."

Her hands were free, so she grabbed the package of cookies and popped it open. She lifted it to her nose and drew in a deep breath. "Heavenly," she said as she closed her eyes, enjoying the sweet and spicy fragrance.

A hand reached around from behind her. "One before I wash dishes." His breath tickled her ear as he spoke. "You should have one, too."

She took another deep breath. That was an even more heavenly scent. Pizza and him. She placed the container of cookies back on the counter and took one out. "Do you have to stand that close to me while you eat?" Henry had not moved away from her as she had expected him to do, and she was enjoying his nearness far too much.

"Sorry," he said as he took a step away.

"We're just friends," she reminded him and herself. See, this was why coming here tonight was a bad idea. She was going to be reminded all night of what she wanted but couldn't have.

"Right. I know. I wasn't thinking. Guess I just got caught up in the moment. Thanks for reminding me."

She studied his face. He didn't look like he was just placating her.

"I mean it. Thanks for reminding me." He leaned a hip against the counter near the sink. "If I do anything to make you uncomfortable, tell me." He popped one half of his cookie in his mouth.

He said the sweetest things. She smiled to herself as she nibbled at her cookie. Most might not think what he had said was sweet, but to her it was. He understood her need to keep him at arm's length even if he didn't understand why.

Henry put the rest of his cookie in his mouth and opened the dishwasher. "This is fun," he said.

"Doing dishes is fun?"

He laughed. "No, but it's nice to have someone to talk to while I do them. Usually, you're in the living room with Brandon or Lacey when you're here. We haven't had much time to talk."

"I'm here now. What do you want to talk about?"

His face scrunched up as he thought. "I don't know. How about how was your day at work? Mine was short. I only had to do some rather boring inventory and ordering stuff. Mother's Day is coming, and I want to make sure we have all the appliances a mom might want her sons to buy her – or I suppose her daughters could buy them, too – but Emma usually buys more girlie stuff than kitchen stuff."

Trish chuckled at that. She imagined a fellow who only knew how to cook pizza well might not be into girlie presents. "We always got Mom flowers, and then, Dad would cook Sunday dinner."

"Do you miss them?"

Trish nodded. "Yeah, despite everything, I do." She shrugged. "I don't know if I should or not, but I do."

"I'd love it if you'd tell me about them sometime."

"There's not much to tell, really. Dad runs the gas station in town, and Mom stays home and does the cooking, cleaning, gardening, all that." She smiled at his lifted eyebrows. "I know it sounds very 1950s, but it works for them." She sighed. "The problem comes when they expect everyone else to hold to the same ideals that they do." She looked down at the floor. "They can be rather critical."

"I figured that out if they didn't think well of you."

"Well, I gave them reason to not think well of me."

"And I gave my parents plenty of reasons to not think well of me." He gave her a pointed look. "I don't want to speak poorly of people I haven't met, but you're their daughter. That should count for something."

"Thanks." She blinked to drive away the tears that wanted to gather. He did say the sweetest things. Maybe Trevor was right. Maybe Henry wouldn't condemn her for her past, but even if he didn't, she still did. "How did you forgive yourself?"

He looked up from attempting to arrange bowls in the dishwasher.

"For everything you did?" she added.

He was silent for a moment while he finally got all the bowls arranged in the dishwasher. "I don't know how I did or even if I have. I guess I did, but I still grieve over what happened. Regrets plague me, ya know?"

"I do." She knew so well.

"And I have to keep placing them at the feet of Jesus almost daily." He put a cup in the dishwasher and then closed the door. "Maybe I should be able to just leave them there and let them go. Maybe one day I will, but for now, I just keep praising Him for loving me despite my faults." The left side of his mouth tipped up into a half-smile. "Grace is not just a word I hear in church anymore and struggle to conceptualize as I once did." He tapped his chest over his heart. "I feel it. I live under it and am wrapped up in it."

"Grace, huh?" Trish smiled. "That's my middle name. Patricia Grace." Maybe she needed to think about that name a bit more if it was what had helped Henry forgive himself.

"It's a beautiful name."

"Thanks."

"Got any other questions that I can fumble around and sort of answer?"

"Not at the moment."

"I have one."

"Okaaay." Did she want to hear it?

"Have you asked God to forgive you for whatever it is?"

She breathed a sigh of relief. That wasn't such a bad question to have to answer. "Yes, many times."

"He forgave you the first time. I have to keep telling myself that. So instead of asking for forgiveness, I thank Him for it and ask Him to help me walk in a way that shows I understand how much He has done for me." He blew out a breath. "Even though I don't deserve it."

"The pizza is smelling good," Fred said as he came into the kitchen. He looked between Henry and Trish. "Am I interrupting?"

"Nah," Henry replied. "We were just talking about forgiveness, and Trish was going to tell me about her day at the library to make waiting for the pizzas go faster."

Fred stuck his head in the fridge. "Cool. Trevor picked an action flick," he said as he came out with three cans of soda.

"He did?" Why would he do that? Trevor knew she didn't like action movies.

Fred shook his head. "No, but I told him I was going to tell you he did. It's a comedy. Today feels like it needs some laughter."

"It does," Trish agreed. "Do you know if Brandon got Gran's laptop set up?"

"Yeah, he did that before he came home. He said she was still slightly loopy from the medication, but the nurse promised to explain how to use it to her."

"I'm glad." Trish pulled out her phone. "I took a picture that I'd like to send her." She opened her photo gallery. "See?" She held the phone so that Fred and Henry could see it. It was a selfie of her with Gran's computer and had *we miss you* written on it."

"Ah, sweet! That's a great idea. We should take some pics tonight and send them over as well." Fred's brow furrowed. "If she was up to it, we could video chat with her, but that might have to wait until tomorrow." He looked at Trish's phone again. "I like it," he said with a nod before wandering back to the living room.

"I like it, too," Henry said. "I wouldn't have thought of doing something like that. I'm not great at sentimental gift ideas."

"You bought my favourite cookies for me."

He shook his head. "That's not a sentimental gift. I wanted this to be a night you would remember with happy thoughts, and food makes me happy."

"I'm still counting it as sentimental." Because it was, even if he didn't think so. He had thought of her and wanted to make her happy. "It was sweet."

"They're cookies. Of course, it's sweet," he teased.

"Fine. I won't accuse you of being sentimental if it makes you uneasy."

He sighed dramatically as if the largest weight in the world had been lifted from his shoulders. "So, how was your day?" He reached behind her for the container of cookies and offered her one before he took one.

"Let me put it this way, people should not be allowed to have teenagers."

Henry barked in laughter. "I think there's no getting around that. Although, having been a troublesome teen, I can understand the sentiment. I shudder to think of parenting someone like me."

"You'll be a great dad," Trish assured him. "And it could be worse. Your kids could all be Brandons." She gave Brandon a teasing look as he entered the kitchen.

"Hey, are you talking about me?" He spotted the container Henry held. "Ooooh, cookies."

Henry wrapped his arm around the container. "I got you oatmeal raisin ones. These are for Trish."

"Oatmeal raisin? Ew. What are those?"

"Not for you," Henry replied.

"This," Trish waved her finger between Henry and Brandon, "is a good depiction of how my two hours with teenagers went."

"Sorry," Henry held the container of cookies towards Brandon. "You can have one of these or one of the oatmeal chocolate chip ones I bought for you."

"Chocolate chips? Not raisins? You're not pranking me, so I take a bite and eat a raisin-infested cookie, are you?"

"No, not today. They're on top of the fridge. Might as well put them on the table." He tucked the cookies he held back in the corner of the counter. "These we'll hide. Want to help me get the chips and stuff out? The pizzas should be done soon."

He was standing too close to her again, but this time, she didn't remind him to move. "Sure, I'll help."

"The bowls I need are in the cupboard behind you."

He reached around her and took down what he needed. "The chips are on the table." Then, with a deep inhale and a sigh, he stepped away from her.

She blew out a breath. *Friends.* That's all they were, and at present, her heart felt as disappointed by that as Henry's sigh had just a moment ago.

Chapter 12

Henry pulled his phone from his pocket and opened the message that had just buzzed its arrival.

Cute, isn't she? Gran's message read.

Below the message was a picture of Trish with Brandon in the background, working on something at his studio. Yeah. Trish was cute. The cutest if you asked him.

Sure is. Brandon not so much. How are you feeling today? Need anything?

Jealousy pricked at Henry's heart as he pressed send and looked again at the photo Gran had sent him. There didn't seem to be any trace of caution in Trish's expression, and he didn't know if that was because she was sending the picture to Gran or if she was just that at ease with Brandon.

I'm feeling pretty good. Gran replied. *Your mom is coming by in a bit to check on me, but I wouldn't be opposed to more company. What are you doing? Working?*

No, not working. Left work a bit ago.

Henry pulled his earbuds out of his ears and stepped off the treadmill. "Hey, Tyler," he called to his workout partner.

"What?" Tyler turned his attention away from reading the tv screen ahead of him and towards Henry.

"Selfie for Gran?" Henry waggled his phone.

"Sure, but do I have to stop? I only have a minute left before cool down."

"Nope. You keep going. I'll just stand here with you over my shoulder." Henry arranged himself to almost look like he was being chased by Tyler and clicked the picture. "Thanks."

"Anything for Gran," Tyler said before going back to watching the tv screen.

Henry hopped back on to his treadmill and sent the picture while continuing the walking portion of today's workout.

Tell Tyler hi.

I will.

Henry waved at Tyler to get his attention. "Gran says hello."

"Has she had any physio yet today?"

Tyler wants to know if you've worked out today with your physiotherapist.

I did that this morning, and when your mom gets here, I plan to walk the hallway a few times with her so she won't start rearranging my kitchen.

Henry chuckled. His mom had been rather insistent that Gran move a few things to make it easier for her to get things done in the kitchen while her hip healed.

"She had physio this morning," he said to Tyler. "I'm going to stretch." Well, he was going to stretch as soon as he sprayed and wiped down the machine.

Emma brought me some healthy muffins. You might like them.

Henry chuckled at that message. *Are you asking me to visit you?*

Yes. Please? I'm not good at being confined.

Next week, you'll get to start doing more.

If I pass all the tests.

He could hear the grumble with which that was likely said. He opened his Bible app, flipped to his recently highlighted verses, copied *Philippians 4:11 I am not saying this because I am in need, for I have learned to be content whatever the circumstances,* and sent it to his grandmother.

Gran replied in a manner some would say was far too immature for her age but exactly how he expected her to reply – with a :P emoji.

He chuckled. *Yeah, contentment is hard.* Did he ever know that! Trish was helping him learn more about that than he wanted to know.

Is that experience talking?

Yep. That's just one of the verses I have been repeating. I've got a few on patience highlighted, too, if you need them.

Haha. No. Just stop by and tell me about it.

There's not much to tell, he replied and then, added, *I'll stop by before I head home. Might be a little sweaty though. So in about half an hour? Is that too soon?*

Not at all. See you then. XO

XO

"I don't see much stretching happening over here." Tyler dropped down on the mat next to Henry.

"I was talking to Gran." He placed his phone on the floor next to him, put the soles of his feet together to get into position for butterfly stretches, and then tapped start on his timer.

"She wants me to come over before I head home," he explained as wrapped his hands around his ankles, leaned forward, and pressed down on his knees with his elbows. "What are you doing after this?"

"Tax documents for a couple of clients. They have to be out before the end of February."

Tyler would be working extra hours from now until the end of April. It was always that way this time of year because he had some clients who only employed his services for tax preparation and others who had him do everything for them.

"I'm planning to stop at the café before I go home," Tyler continued. "Cari offered to drop off their financial stuff when she got home tonight, but I'd rather get it earlier than that. Have you stopped by there lately? It's looking good."

"No, I haven't. I suppose I should."

"Online orders are bringing in some good revenue. They should be ready to hire some more staff by the time school lets out for them. They're just waiting on my confirmation of their calculations before moving ahead with their plans, which is why I would like to pick up their stuff sooner rather than later. I know Emma said she was anxious for my opinion."

"Just Emma?" Henry shot his friend a suspicious look.

"Emma was the one who called to say Cari would drop things off to me. I'm sure Cari is just as anxious, but I didn't talk to Cari. I talked to Emma." Tyler leaned into a hamstring stretch. "It's pretty impressive what those two have been able to accomplish in such a short time. I can't divulge all I know, of course, but God is blessing them for following His leading in this."

Henry couldn't help but smile at the news that his sister was doing well. "How could they do poorly? I've always enjoyed Emma's cooking, and Cari's stuff nearly outshines it. But don't tell Emma I said that." He laughed.

"She would agree. I don't think she'd be offended at all," Tyler said as he rose to join Henry in doing some standing stretches.

That was true. Emma wasn't the sort to feel threatened by the abilities of her friends, especially Cari. Those two were nearly inseparable. They didn't just work and go to school together. They seemed to do everything together.

"So, by summer, they'll have the café, the food truck, and online orders?" Henry asked.

Tyler nodded.

"And they'll stay financially afloat?"

Again, Tyler nodded. "As long as they stick to the plan they have in place."

"The one you have to double-check?"

"Yep, and the one that Will will look at after I'm done."

Right, that made sense. Will had invested in Emma and Cari's venture from the beginning and had signed on to be their business mentor for as long as they needed him. That, in and of itself, nearly guaranteed that the café business would be a success. There were very few things that Will got involved with that didn't turn a profit or, at the least, break even. Henry's eldest and closest brother was detail oriented, nearly to the point of obsessive.

"You'll still have room in your schedule to do my taxes?" Henry asked.

"Always. Nothing on my part will ever change that."

"Awesome. I'd hate to have to find a new accountant."

"I just picked up Brandon as a client yesterday."

Henry laughed. "You'll soon know all the financial matters of the Bennett clan."

Tyler joined Henry in laughing. "Actually, I already do."

"What? You do?"

Tyler nodded. "Brandon was the last hold out."

"Edmund has you do his taxes?"

"Ever since he started doing the editing thing. He said he wasn't comfortable figuring out all the business stuff. If he was only doing personal taxes, he'd still be doing his own."

Fred had been getting someone to do his taxes for him since he started working. For a few years back in high school, that someone had been Eddie. Then, college had happened for them both, and Fred had been going to one of those pop-up tax places each year until Tyler got his certification.

"It sounds like you might need to hire some staff."

"That's the plan for next year."

"Seriously? What happened to keeping it a work from home business?"

"I want a bigger home without a brother in it." Tyler chuckled. "I'd like to get married at some point, and it would be good to have enough money to support a family."

Henry nodded. "A family would be nice." He had always known he wanted to one day have a family.

"You'll have one," Tyler assured him.

Henry blew out a breath. "I'm trusting God that I will." And after a couple of nights ago when Trish had come over for pizza, his desire to have her as part of that future family had been what had driven him to start reading verses about contentment and patience.

"Done?" he asked Tyler, who was picking up his shoes and about to walk sock-footed over to where their bags were stashed.

"Yep. You?"

"In ten seconds." Henry watched his timer count down as he held a shoulder stretch. "There. Done." He turned off the alarm as a message popped up on his phone.

"Is that Gran again?" Tyler asked.

Henry shook his head. "It's Trish." It was the second time in as many days that he had gotten a text from her for no reason other than to say hi and tell him what she was doing.

"Hey." Tyler gave Henry's shoulder a thump. "That's good, right?"

"Yeah, I think so." He turned the screen to show Tyler the picture Trish had sent him. "I'd think it was a better thing if it wasn't a text to tell me about this bowl Brandon made or repaired or whatever you want to say."

"What do you mean?" Tyler took Henry's phone. "Kintsugi? What is that?"

Henry shrugged. "I guess it's whatever Brandon did to fix that bowl." And make it look beautiful. "I thought he was just good at photography, but since he decided to open that studio, he's really becoming versatile." It was almost as if his decision to step out on his own had opened a floodgate of creativity in him.

"He's going to burn something." Tyler handed Henry's phone back to him. On the screen, was a picture of Brandon with a small blow torch.

"Someone should make sure he has the right sort of insurance for his business."

"I doubt your brother is going to burn down his place of business and future home. When does he move out of your place?"

"Next week."

"That's earlier than expected!"

"Yeah, he's anxious to be on his own again and thinks he can get things set up better and faster if he's on site."

"Makes sense."

Don't let him burn down his house. Henry texted.

Haha. Very funny. He seems to know what he's doing, and there's a bucket of water next to him. This bowl is beautiful. It was just a cheap second-hand store purchase that he broke and then put back together. Who knew that broken stuff could become so beautiful?

Henry's lips tipped up into a half-smile. "Brandon and God," he said as he typed those words to send to Trish.

"What is Brandon and God?" Tyler looked over Henry's shoulder at his phone.

Henry shrugged. "An object lesson that I hope Trish will get without me having to unravel it all and look like a church-going know-it-all."

"But you are," Tyler teased as he moved toward the door of the gym.

"Maybe, but I'd rather not look like one." Especially when his brother was making beautiful artwork and looking cool using a propane torch to burn wood.

"Still jealous of him, huh?"

Leave it to Tyler to not ignore the obvious.

"Yeah, a bit."

"She's with him and texting you." Tyler pulled up the hood on his jacket.

"She's with him," Henry repeated.

"And texting you. Stop worrying about him."

"I know you're right, and I know being jealous is stupid. But I can't seem to stop being stupid."

Tyler chuckled. "Yeah, love does that, I hear. Tell Gran hi."

"I will."

It's going to be a shelf. He's going to scorch the wood, then stain it, and make it into a shelf. The burning thing is called Shou Sugi Ban.

Another thing of beauty made from something that was damaged. Henry climbed into his car. "Let her see the symbolism," he prayed.

Both the bowl thing and the wood thing are Japanese and require destruction before they become beautiful. Therefore, Bennett, your answer should have been the Japanese, Brandon, and God.

I apologize for my error. *happy face*

So you're not perfect. I'm ok with that.

Glad to hear it. When will the shelf be done?

He says tomorrow. Maybe. He'll send me a pic once it's finished.

Share it with me?

Of course.

Henry started his car and put it into gear. His phone buzzed with another message.

Kind of comforting to know that even damaged stuff can be used to make something pretty, huh?

She got it. He closed his eyes and thanked God for that. Then, he typed, *Excessively. Heading to Gran's.*

See you there.

See him there? He put his car back in park.

Gran, are you meddling? Is Trish coming over to your house?

Henry tapped his steering wheel in time to the music playing on the radio while he waited for a reply from his grandmother. It wasn't too long in coming.

Yes and yes. I love you.

He shook his head and smiled at her reply. She was such a sweet schemer.

Thanks. But don't tell Mom I'm ok with this. I love you, too. Do I have time to shower?

You can use my shower if you want, but she knows you were at the gym.

How?

I sent her that picture of you and Tyler. I asked her the same question I asked you about her pic, and I got nearly the same reply. Only she didn't mention Brandon or Tyler.

We're just friends. He blew out a breath. Not that he didn't want to be more and suspected he always would. *But I love her.*

So do I, and she needs our love.

Do you know her secret? I'm not asking you to tell me it. I just want to know exactly how wise you are being or if you're just guessing.

Do I ever just guess?

Does that mean you know her secret?

Yes, Henry, I do. She NEEDS our love. Trust me. She'll tell you when she's ready and not too terrified of being rejected. Do you hear what I am saying?

Do you think I would reject her?

No, but she might. She thought I would once I heard her story, or the parts of it she told me. Just love her, Henry. Just love her.

I don't think I have any other choice, Gran. See you soon. XO

XO

Henry smiled at the familiar symbols of love that always signaled that he and Gran were done texting. Someday, if he stayed his course and God blessed, he hoped to sign all his texts to Trish the same way.

Chapter 13

"Did you have a good run?" Trish dropped her bag next to Gran's door and slipped off her shoes.

"Yeah, I did," Henry answered. "It looked like you and Brandon were enjoying yourselves."

Hmm. She couldn't hear any jealousy in that comment, which was good. She and Brandon were just friends – and not like she and Henry were. There was no tingle when Brandon touched her. No charged air between them when they were close. No desire to be anything more than just friends. And that was exactly the opposite of how her friendship with Henry was.

She shrugged out of her coat. "We took a walk, and then went back to his studio so he could work on those projects I showed you."

Her first impulse after hearing about the broken bowl and seeing it fixed in such a beautiful way was to share it with Henry. Oh, she was in such trouble when it came to him. No matter how she tried to keep her heart from wishing for more than a friendship, it simply wouldn't listen. Her heart longed to be free of her past more now than ever before.

"I thought you didn't do outside in the winter because of ice?"

"I don't *run* outside in the winter because of ice, and it was above freezing today, just like it was yesterday. There is far less ice than there was. In fact..." She paused to give Gran's cheek a kiss. "The trail we took today was nearly clear. It's the one over by Friendly's." She sat down on the edge of the sofa closest to where Gran was propped up in her recliner. "How are you feeling?"

"The pain meds they have me on are worth their weight in gold," Gran replied with a wink and a chuckle. "Actually, I find I'm taking less of them each day. I'm happy to see you. Both of you," she added with a smile for her grandson. "Henry is making us a hot drink." She leaned forward and dropped her voice to a stage whisper that Trish was sure she wanted Henry to hear. "He heard I like those mocha pods, and he stopped on the way here to make sure I had enough of them."

"He's sweet like that," Trish agreed. "Do you know what he made sure to have at his place the other night when Trevor and I were over for pizza and a movie?"

Gran studied Henry who shrugged. He didn't seem bothered at all that he was the topic of discussion. In fact, he looked like he enjoyed it.

"I'm sure I can't guess," Gran finally replied.

"Ginger snaps," Trish whispered.

"Indeed?" Gran looked far too excited about that. "And were they good?"

"Delicious. I ate at least half a dozen of them."

"She really likes them." Henry drew out the word *really*.

Gran chuckled. "I have a recipe for them. The two of you should come over and make some for me one day. I'd make them myself, but then, the nurse, my daughter, my physio, and likely anyone else who heard about it would scold me. I've been told no baking until the doctor clears me for more activity."

"I'm not very good at baking, Gran," Henry cautioned from where he stood leaning against the wall that divided the kitchen from the hallway.

"You do just fine when someone helps you focus, and I think having a pretty girl there to tell you what to do would make focusing rather easy."

"Gran!" Trish said at the same time Henry did.

Gran just laughed. "I know. I know. Just you're just *friends*." She put air quotes around the word friends. She reached over and patted Trish's knee. "But I'm still praying. Now, get comfy on that couch and tell me everything I am missing by being held captive in my home while Henry gets the muffins and mochas."

"Are you sure he doesn't need help?" Trish asked. "It is three mugs and a container of muffins."

"I can handle it," Henry called from the kitchen.

"You're sure?" Trish called back.

"Positive," came the reply.

A sliver of disappointment flickered through Trish as she shifted back on the couch and pulled her right foot under her. She had kind of hoped for one of those close contact kitchen moments with him like they had had at his place. She shouldn't want that, but she did.

"Your computer at the library has had company," Trish said to Gran. "You got that picture I sent you, right?"

Yesterday, Trish had asked the young woman, who had come into the library to work on a writing project, if she could take a picture of her and send it to the lady who usually used that computer but was at home recovering from surgery.

"That same girl was there again?"

"She was. Her name is Ava, and she seems really sweet." Trish glanced toward the kitchen. Henry was still nowhere to be seen, which was good since she did not want him to hear this part. "I caught her checking out Eddie more than once."

Gran's brow rose. "Is she single?"

Trish nodded. "I asked a few questions." Because she had known Gran would want details.

"Does she go to church?"

Again, Trish nodded. "They are doing some remodeling to the library in Wilson's Crossing, which is where she usually goes to write, but some lady named Doreen, whom she goes to church with and who works at the city offices, suggested she try the Hatfield Falls library. She lives with her sister, Ali, and her sister has a dog that likes to bark and a baby, Riley, that likes to cry, so writing can be challenging in that environment."

"What does she write?"

"She says she does some freelance stuff and also writes fiction. She was a bit reluctant to admit to what sort of fiction she wrote so I didn't push it." However, she had seen some familiar romance novels in Ava's bag.

"Maybe if you get to know her better." Gran's tone was somewhat disappointed to not know all the details about a girl who showed interest in her grandson. "But you said she was looking at Eddie?"

"Yep, and I can't blame her. He's cute. I used to watch him just for the pleasure of something handsome to look at." There were two other guys that worked with her at the library, but neither of them were as good-looking as Eddie.

"Used to?"

"Yeah, used to," Trish answered as Henry came into the room with two cups.

He placed one on the table next to Gran and the other on the coffee table in front of Trish and looked between her and Gran. "Do you want me to take my time in the kitchen getting the muffins so you can continue to discuss whatever it was you were discussing?"

"I don't know what you mean," his grandmother said with a grin.

"I heard voices in here as I was getting things ready, but as soon as I stepped into the room, you stopped talking. I might not be as smart as Will or Edmund, but I do know what that means."

"Oh, you're every bit as smart as any of your brothers," Gran assured him. "And yes, just hang back a little. Trish was about to answer my question."

"I already did," Trish said. She really did *not* want to say anything more about why she didn't watch Eddie like she used to.

"Not satisfactorily, and I'm an old, injured woman who shouldn't be stressed unnecessarily."

Henry laughed. "I see your ability to rationalize your way into getting to know what you want to know has not been damaged." He looked at Trish. "So, do I take my time or not?"

"You'd really provoke your grandmother for me?" Again, it was not one of those things most might think of as sweet, but she did. Oh! Why did she have to fall in love with him more and more with each lovely thing he said or did? This was why she should have kept her distance from him.

"I would." He held her gaze. "It's your call. I know how demanding she can be."

"Demanding, indeed!" Gran cried as if offended. Her expression, however, did not support her tone of voice, for she looked rather pleased to have been called demanding.

"I guess you can take your time. She is injured."

"If that's what you want." He didn't move.

"It's what I need," she answered. It was only then, that he took himself back to the kitchen.

"He loves you," Gran whispered.

Trish kept her eyes fixed on the entry to the kitchen. "And I..." she paused. Could she truly admit this? There would be no going back after it was said.

"You what?" Gran prodded.

Trish looked at Barb, the lady who had stood in a cold alleyway and had adopted her as her granddaughter without reservation and had continued to love her even after knowing about her past. She could tell her. Her secret would be safe.

"I love him." She shrugged. "That's why I can't watch Eddie anymore. I started to stop when Lacey mentioned her handsy boss and how my flirting reminded her of that, but then, Henry..." She wasn't quite sure how to put the rest of what was in her heart into words. "But you know I can't be more than friends with him."

"You could be. The only one stopping you is yourself."

Trish shook her head. It wasn't that easy. Was it? "How can I?"

"Henry, dear."

Trish sucked in a deep breath. Barb wasn't going to tell him, was she? She wouldn't, would she? Gran was different than her parents and the people at her old church, wasn't she?"

"Is it safe to come back?" he asked from inside the kitchen.

"Not quite, dear. I just wanted you to share your second favourite verse with us."

His second favourite verse? Did people actually have those?

Henry appeared at the kitchen entry. "But I can't come back? There are currently three muffins here, but I make no promises that there will be enough for everyone if I am left here too long. I did just run three miles."

"Just tell me your second favourite verse, and then, we'll see if you can join us or not."

Henry blew out a breath. "Okay, here goes. Romans 8: 1 *Therefore, there is now no condemnation for those who are in Christ Jesus.*"

"And why is there no condemnation?"

"Can't I answer that while sitting?" He looked from Gran to Trish. "I promise to leave if needed."

"Can you tell me what you need to if he does join us?"

Gran nodded. "I think I can."

Trish patted the sofa next to her.

Henry smiled, ducked back into the kitchen, and reappeared with a plate of muffins and a mug of mocha.

"There is no condemnation," he said as he put his cup on the coffee table and then made sure Gran had a muffin, "because Christ bore all the condemnation for everyone when He died on the cross."

"You mean even the condemnation that might come with messing up after you're one of His children?" Gran asked.

"I do." He placed the remaining muffins on the coffee table and took a seat next to Trish.

"You just need to believe that," Gran said to Trish.

"But..." It seemed as if there must be something she had to do to regain God's grace. There were things she would have to do to be accepted back into her family or old church. Not that she wanted to be accepted into her old church, but she might want to see her parents again. She picked up her mug of mocha. "That's it?"

Gran nodded. "God doesn't condemn you, so why should you condemn yourself?"

Trish glanced nervously at Henry.

"I'm not going to ask what you did," he assured her. "You'll tell me when you're ready."

"You keep saying that, but I may never be ready."

He took a bite of his muffin and nodded. "I know, and I'm trying to make peace with that." His lips tipped into a half-smile.

The room sat in silence for a minute. It was as if both Henry and his grandmother were waiting for her to speak before they said anything, but she didn't know what to say.

She wasn't sure if she was able to believe that restoration was so simple.

"I didn't know that people had more than one favourite verse." That seemed a good way to avoid having to decide about believing what Gran said or not. She broke off a piece of muffin.

"I don't know if everyone does, but I do," Henry said. "And they haven't always been the same verses. I find God gives me new ones to hold onto at different points. However, I doubt my first favourite will ever be relegated to second or third or fourth."

"Why's that?"

"Because it's what keeps me moving forward and living in forgiveness and not thinking I have to do something to earn God's approval."

That piqued Trish's interest even if it did bring her right back into the place she was trying to avoid. "Yeah? What is it?"

"It's two verses actually. Romans 8 verses 38 and 39."

Trish gasped. "Oh, I know those." She pulled out her phone and opened her picture gallery. "These." She clicked on the image of one of the pages in the notebook Gran had given her.

Henry took her phone from her. He smiled as he read the verses. "Yep, that's them. Nothing can separate us from God's love. Not even my wild partying days."

"You have those verses on your phone?" Gran asked leaning her head forward as if that would help her see what Henry was looking at.

"I took a picture of the page you wrote in my notebook, so I could have it with me as a reminder that you promised to always love me." Her cheeks felt warm.

"And I will. Do you believe that?"

Trish nodded as she savoured the cinnamon apple goodness of her muffin.

"You do know that God is more trustworthy than even me, right?" Gran asked her.

Trish lowered her muffin without taking the bite she had planned to take. "I suppose I do know that."

"Your family and church taught you not to trust God because they required you to earn their love."

Gran was always direct. Trish both liked and disliked that about her. She didn't give you anywhere to hide. She just shone her light right into the dark corners and exposed what needed to be seen.

"God's not like that," she added. "His love is a gift."

Trish flipped a couple of pictures over. "Yeah, you wrote that as well." She handed her phone to Gran who took it and increased the size of the image.

"What's this written in purple here?"

Trish cringed. "I hope you won't be angry that I wrote in the notebook."

"*Best gift ever*?" Gran smiled. "I couldn't be mad at my love for you being called that. However, my love is nothing compared to God's and hopefully, one day, your husband's."

Trish put her half-eaten muffin on the plate and blew out a breath. She was going to cry again. Barb was constantly making her feel so vulnerable and cared for. "But it was your love that opened my eyes to the possibility of God still loving me." She brushed a tear from her cheek.

"Then, my dear girl, I am happy to have my love called the best gift ever, for if you can even begin to embrace the length and breadth of the love that God has for you, it will heal your heart, and you will have that husband you keep telling me you'll never have." Her eyes flicked to Henry. "And you know who I hope that is."

Trish pulled the corner of her bottom lip between her teeth as she smiled to hide her discomfort at having the subject of her and Henry spoken of so openly.

"I know who I hope it is."

Henry's words drew Trish's attention. He wanted to marry her? That was an enormous step from wanting to date her – which she already knew was his desire.

"I know we're just friends," he continued, "but I'm not going to lie about what I wish we were. Gran already knows."

The door to Gran's apartment began to open.

"But don't tell my mom," Henry hissed as that very woman entered.

"That girl's timing was never good," Gran muttered, causing Trish to chuckle nervously.

"Have I frightened you into hiding again?" Henry whispered to her.

Trish shook her head and then shrugged. "I don't think so."

"Oh, you have company," Mrs. Bennet said as she entered the living room. "Trish, it's good to see you."

"And me, Mom? Is it good to see me?" Henry asked as he stood and moved around the coffee table to give his mother a hug.

"You know it is, sweetie." She looked at the plate on the table. "Are those Emma's apple muffins?"

"They are, and they're so good." Trish picked up what remained of her muffin.

"There are still three in the container in the kitchen. Do you want me to get you one?" Henry asked.

"No, I'm capable, but thank you."

"Do not rearrange anything while you're in there," Gran called after her.

"I already told you I wouldn't."

"Yes, but what you say and what you do are sometimes opposites." Gran looked at Trish. "She doesn't mean to say one thing and do another, it just happens. An idea pops into her head, and she's done it before she knows she's started."

"I suppose she needed to be able to do some things without much thought when her kids were little," Trish offered.

"Especially after Henry was born." Gran winked at him. "He was trouble from the start."

"Hey, I'm not trouble now."

"Most days you're not, but I have heard about your pranks. Remind me again how you sprained your ankle last year."

Henry's eyes narrowed. "Nope. Not going there."

Trish shot him a curious look.

"I fell escaping from Tyler and Blake's place. The ladder had one more rung than I remembered it had."

"Why were you escaping?"

He grimaced. "Blake and I played a trick on Tyler, and he didn't find it as funny as we did."

"You really are trouble, aren't you?" Trish asked with a laugh.

He grinned and settled back on the couch with his mocha in his hand. Was it her imagination, or had he moved closer to her? Yeah, he was trouble. T-R-O-U-B-L-E in a handsome package who held her broken and wary heart, even if he didn't know it. What was she going to do about that?

Chapter 14

"Taking attendance?" Blake sidled up to Henry, who was watching the door to the youth room at the church where the singles night was happening this month. Thankfully, his mother had not been successful in her quest to have February's activity be a Valentine's banquet. Instead, they were going to play games, watch some old movie, and have a time of worship – and not on Valentine's Day.

"Nope. Just waiting for someone."

"Hey, Princess." Blake doffed his imaginary top hat to Cari as she entered.

"Peasant," she said with a pointed look and a scowl.

Blake chuckled. "She likes me. She just pretends not to."

"Yeah, I'm not so sure about that," Henry said.

"She hasn't slashed the tires on my truck, and she says *hello* when I see her at the apartment building."

"I'm still not sure that means she likes you."

Blake shrugged. "It's good enough for me. Now, who are we watching for?"

"Trish. She said she'd come tonight."

"Yeah? That's kind of a big deal for her, isn't it?"

"It is." Trish had been coming to church for several months now, but tonight was the first singles night she had agreed to attend.

Henry checked his phone. "I haven't gotten any messages telling me she can't make it."

He had honestly been expecting one all day. After all, he had told her at Gran's three days ago that he wanted to marry her, and she still wasn't past the "we're just friends" phase. While she had said he hadn't scared her away, he wasn't so sure she wasn't going to change her mind on that.

"Text her," Blake suggested when Henry looked at his phone again. "She's probably just running late."

Or just running – as far away from him as she could go. His phone buzzed.

"Maybe that's her." Blake looked over Henry's shoulder. "Freddie? What's he want?"

"He says that he and Trish will be here soon." That was odd. Trish had refused to ride with him when he had asked her if he could pick her up, and now she was coming with Fred? What was up with that? Was she just avoiding him where she could? That was likely it. He should probably just be happy that it wasn't Brandon who was with her.

You and Trish? he typed to Fred.

Flat tire.

She called.

I fixed.

Fred's brief replies pinged in one after the other.

"She had a flat tire," he said to Blake who was still looking over his shoulder.

"Yep, I can see that." He nudged Henry's arm with his arm when another message popped up on Henry's screen. "Well, that's good news. Might actually be another Bennett wedding in the future if things keep going as they are."

Henry shook his head. "Not if Trish is the one you expect to marry a Bennett brother. She's still not ready for that. She won't even date me, and we should probably go on at least one date before we get married."

However, it was nice to see Fred's message about Trish being worried about being late and about Henry wondering if she was coming or not. He might have a chance with her at some point. Of course, she hadn't texted him about her tire or her worry about being late. He rubbed the back of his neck. Having patience and being understanding was not easy.

"I wouldn't worry too much," Blake said. "You managed to get me to come to church and to Christ. If you could do that, then, I'd put my money on you being successful with Trish."

"Thanks, man. I appreciate the confidence." And he hoped Blake was right.

"We're just about ready to start," Mandy Mitchell said. "You might want to stake out a good board game before they're all taken, and you're left with checkers."

Henry had known Mandy from the time he could remember any of the kids in his Sunday school class. She was a year younger than him so she had been in Blake's class in school, but at church, several age groups were lumped together with one teacher. She had followed him around back in elementary school, but she had stopped paying much attention to him in high school. She was a good girl who didn't want to associate with anyone she would consider bad, and he had been on the bad list in high school. However, since he had sorted out his standing with the Lord, she had once again been showing him marked attention – attention he didn't want. She was a pretty girl and nice and all, but she was Mandy.

"Thanks for the heads up, but I have a friend coming, so I'll wait."

"I could save you a seat," Mandy offered with a sweet smile.

"That's a kind offer, but I'll take my chances."

Her smile slipped into a pout.

What twenty-five-year-old woman pouted? It was one of the many things about Mandy that did nothing to endear her to him.

"So, you're waiting for Trish."

"I am." For as long as it took, he would wait for her – and not just so they could play games together tonight – he'd wait for her to be ready to love him for as long as it took, though he did hope it wouldn't take forever.

"We were afraid of that," Mandy admitted with a sigh.

"What do you mean, *we*?" And what was she afraid of? She said it as if she thought he was once again walking down the devil's road hand and hand with Satan himself.

"Tiffany, Esther, and me." Mandy looked around and lowered her voice. "Trish seems to get around." She gave him a look that said she expected him to understand that Trish was not the sort of girl she would approve of.

If she had ever hoped to sway him to like her, she had just put the last nail in that coffin. However, before he could say anything, Blake had taken up Trish's cause.

"She's not like that," Blake said. "She's just friendly."

"But she hangs out with Brandon and his brothers and you and your brother, and she has Henry following her around," Mandy protested. "I haven't seen her with any ladies from the church except Lacey and sometimes Emma and Cari. What's up with that?"

"What's up with what?" Blake retorted. "She hangs out with the people who hang out with her. Have you gone out of your way to do things with her?"

"Well, no," Mandy stammered.

"Exactly." Blake folded his arms and glared at Mandy. "You're just jealous because Henry here is off the market, and it wasn't you who took him off the market."

"Is he?" Mandy's cheeks were crimson, and her eyes were flashing.

Blake had that affect on people, but at present, Henry had no desire to douse the fire burning in front of him. He was too busy biting his tongue to keep from saying a few things he might later regret and make Trish uncomfortable.

"Are you and Trish dating, then?" Mandy asked him.

"No, but I'd like for us to be."

"Then, what's the hold up? Can't she decide which Bennett brother to like best?" She gave a flick of her head and would have marched away if Henry hadn't grabbed her arm.

"Listen, Mandy. Trish isn't what you're saying. She's not. Not at all." He shook his head. How did he say this without divulging things he didn't want to? "You love God, right?"

Mandy's brow furrowed. "Yeah."

"Then, act like it."

Despite Henry's soft tone, Mandy still recoiled as if he had slapped her.

"We don't know everyone's story, Mandy. You don't know Trish's." He didn't even know Trish's story. "There might be a reason she finds it hard to trust others." He blew out a breath and shook his head. He knew she struggled with that. He just didn't know why. "Please, just be kind to her tonight. Don't push her away from God." And away from him.

Mandy's head tipped, and she studied him for a minute before she nodded. "Fine. I wasn't planning to be rude to her anyway." Her eyes flicked to Blake. "You might want to use the same speech on your friend here."

"You accused her of *things*," Blake said.

Mandy nodded. "You're right, and I apologize."

"Apology accepted, and I shall try to be less abrasive for the rest of the evening."

"Yeah, right," Mandy muttered.

"I said try," Blake retorted.

Mandy smiled a saccharine smile at Blake and fluttered her lashes. "I suppose it was sweet how you came to Trish's defense."

"I am not sweet," he called after her. "Don't be telling people that."

Mandy turned back and simply shrugged before continuing on her way to a table where Tiffany and Esther were waiting for her.

"She's going to tell them I'm sweet," Blake grumbled.

"And knowing what they know about you, do you really think they'll believe her?" Henry asked.

Blake's brow furrowed. "I suppose not."

"Then, your secret is safe. You may go be your caustic self without fear of anyone knowing that you have a heart lurking behind your beastly façade."

Blake rolled his eyes. "You've been hanging around a chick that likes books far too much."

"Nah," Henry said, "I'd say I don't get to spend nearly enough time with her." Of course, anything less than every day for the rest of his life was less than enough time with her. He checked his phone again. The activity would start in three minutes.

"She'll be here soon," Blake assured him. "Should I go claim us a table? I'll make sure there's enough room for Trish and Fred to join us."

"Make sure it has enough for Trish and me. Fred can fend for himself. Mandy has an empty chair at her table."

"Offering your little brother up as a peace offering?" Blake asked with a laugh.

"If I have to." And Fred wouldn't mind sitting at a table full of ladies, especially if one of those ladies was Esther.

As Blake walked over to the game tables, the door to the youth room opened, and Fred and Trish walked in.

"Finally." Henry breathed a sigh of relief.

"I'm sorry I was so late." Trish came directly to him. "I called Fred since I knew from Eddie he wasn't working today, but I knew you were, and your house is closer to my house than Drummonds is." She stopped and bit her lip.

"I'm just glad you're here." Henry looked over her head to Freddie. "Thanks for helping her out."

"Any time. She's going to need to get that spare replaced with a good tire as soon as possible. She shouldn't be driving on it too much."

"You drove here?"

"Fred followed me."

"Why didn't you just ride with him?"

Fred chuckled, as if that was a conversation he had already been part of, and with a wave left Henry and Trish alone.

"I'm scared," Trish whispered. "I don't know if I can stay the whole time. I needed a way to go home early."

Henry wanted to take her hand and reassure her that things were going to be fine. However, he had heard Mandy earlier, and he knew he couldn't take Trish's hand or honestly promise that all would be okay. So, he didn't.

"If you need to leave, let me follow you home to make sure you get there. Or better yet, let me know, we'll drop your car off at your place, and I'll treat you to some ice cream at the Falls Diner."

"But you like these things, don't you?"

Henry looked around the room and nodded. He really did enjoy getting together with church friends and having a good time. It reminded him somewhat of the fun that had been part of his partying life. It was not a good way to live for someone who wanted to follow God – or probably anyone in general – but there were aspects of it that had been quite enjoyable – mainly, the getting together with friends part.

"I do," he admitted. "But I like you more." And that was the truth. If he had to choose between spending time with his church friends and her tonight, he'd choose her. And the replying smile she gave him – the kind he had only ever seen her give her brother until now – well, that was something he would do anything to continue to see.

"Blake is saving us a couple of spots at a table, so we don't end up playing checkers." They started to cross the room to where Blake stood next to a table.

"But I like checkers," she teased.

"Oh, it'd be fun for the first game, but after three or four games in a row, it might get boring."

"I suppose, but there are other games you can play with a checkerboard besides just checkers. I know because I shelved a book about it today."

"But do you know how to play any of them?" He pulled out her chair for her.

"It was a children's book, so I'm going to guess I could figure it out, and I have a phone with internet searching capability." She retorted with another completely happy smile for him.

"Then, maybe we should take one of those checkerboards."

"You're not moving," Blake said. "I had to fight off a scourge of people to save those seats for you. You'll stay and play *Dutch Blitz*, and you'll enjoy it."

Trish chuckled. "If you say we must, then, I guess we must." She turned toward Cari. "Did he insist that you and Emma play with him, too?"

Cari laughed. "No, that was Emma's doing. I would've happily taken a seat somewhere else." She sighed. "But I do look forward to beating him, so it's not all bad."

"Hey, I'll have you know I'm the *Dutch Blitz* king, Princess," Blake protested.

"Can't you please call her Cari for tonight?" Emma begged.

"But she looks like a princess with her pretty pink hair."

"Is that why you call her that?"

"Yeah, and she seemed a little precious about a parking spot that once."

Cari huffed. "I'm not precious."

Blake lifted and lowered one shoulder. "Maybe you are, maybe you're not."

"Blake," Tyler snapped. "I'll tell her your middle name."

"Fine. I'll attempt to call her Cari even if I like Princess better."

Blake pushed everyone to the edge of their tolerance and some people beyond it. However, when his brother snapped and threatened the middle name thing, Blake knew he was beaten.

"Oh, that sounds intriguing," Trish said. "I think I'd like to hear what this middle name is, wouldn't you, Cari?"

"Oh, most certainly," Cari agreed. "However, if not knowing means I don't have to be called Princess, I think I can live with the curiosity. At least, for now."

"If it means a truce between you and Blake," Emma said, "I can pretend to not care one bit what his middle name might be, but I bet it's something very un-Blake like."

"Very," Henry assured them.

"You know it?" All three ladies asked him at once.

"I sure do, but I'm not divulging it because I'm good at keeping secrets." He made a point of looking at Trish when he said that last part. How he wished she'd trust her secrets to him. Then, he might be better able to help her move forward. As it was, he'd just have to trust Gran to use what she knew to guide Trish – and him.

"I made no promise to never tell what it is, and I'll share it if needed," Tyler added with a pointed look for his brother.

"I already said I'd try not to call her Princess."

"Remind me to book a hair appointment," Cari said to Emma.

"Why?" Emma asked.

"So I can change the colour of my hair."

"What?" Blake asked in shock. "Why do you want to change it? You look good in pink."

"Because I'm not a princess."

Blake scowled at her. "Will you keep the hair if I promise not to call you Princess for like... a week?"

Cari shook her head.

"What colour will you change it to?" Emma asked.

"I don't know. Maybe I'll go back to my normal brown. The pink is getting a little old now."

"Normal brown?" Blake squinted at her. "Yeah, that might look good, too."

"Might?" Cari shot back.

"Well, I can't be certain if I haven't seen it." Blake shuffled the deck of cards and started dealing them out. "You could try purple. I kind of like purple."

Henry was pretty sure that whatever colour Blake suggested was going to be the one colour Cari would refuse to get, and yet, somehow, Blake thought that Cari liked him. It was more like she tolerated him when forced.

"Have you ever thought about colouring your hair?" he asked Trish.

"Never."

"Good." He held her gaze. "I think the colour God gave you is perfect."

"Hey, we're trying to play a game here," Blake said. "You can stare into Trish's eyes later."

"Shut up, Blake," Henry retorted as he turned his attention to his cards. He'd love to stare into Trish's eyes later if she'd let him, and tonight, it almost seemed as if she might.

Chapter 15

"Hey, how was the activity last night?" Lacey came behind the front desk at the library to retrieve the things she needed for the mom and tots time she was running today.

"I survived." It hadn't been as bad as Trish had expected it to be.

"Did you stay the whole time?"

"I did." She had been surprised at how comfortable she had felt hanging out with Henry and his group of friends. There were a few at the games night who had looked at her with an expression that said they wondered if she was good enough for them or not, but Blake, Tyler, Emma, and Cari had been great. "Cari is pretty cool."

Last night had been the first time Trish had spent much time with Lacey's younger sister. It was easier to stay disconnected in larger groups like when everyone gathered at Lacey's place, but last night, having been seated at a table with so few, Trish had been required to connect. What she had found had surprised her.

"You don't have to convince me of that." Lacey sat down next to Trish and placed her bag of toys and books on her lap. "She said something to me when I talked to her last night that I think you should know, because I think you really helped her."

Trish's eyes grew wide at that. She had helped Cari some how? "What did she say?"

"She said that when you were talking about guys, and she mentioned that she discovered her ex had another girl-friend, whom, I believe, she called a colourful name."

Trish chuckled. "She sure did, and it might be a fitting name." Even if it was not the sort of word one normally heard inside a church.

"Well, when you were talking about him, you told her that the other woman might not have known she was the other woman because if he's lying to you, there's a good chance that he's also lying to her. She said that really struck her. She hadn't thought about that as a possibility, and she feels like she can let go of part of her anger over the whole situation."

Trish remembered how startled Cari had looked when she had said that. "I'm glad it was helpful."

Lacey glanced around them and then leaned forward. "Is that what happened to you? Did some guy cheat on you? If so, it makes how upset you were about Will hiding our relationship make even more sense."

Trish held her friend's gaze for a moment without reply-ing. Could she answer that question honestly? Her heart raced at the thought of doing so, but something told her that she could trust Lacey with this. She shook her head. "Not exactly. It turns out I was the other woman."

"Oh," the word came out in a breath. "And you had no idea, huh?"

"Not a clue until I went to visit him and found out he had a wife. But other than Gran, no one here knows about that." There were several who knew about it back in Foster's Arm, but not here.

"I won't share what you have said." Lacey's brow furrowed and concern etched her features. "That must be a heavy weight to bear. I'm so sorry that happened to you."

There was no condemnation in her friend's voice. There was only genuine care and love.

"It is heavy," Trish admitted, "and not something I have yet been able to get over."

"Forgive me for being too curious, but is that why you think you can never get married? Not all men lie to the women they say they love. I know Henry would never lie to you." She glanced at her watch as the door opened, and a mom and her daughter entered. "And I'm sure he wouldn't hold that part of your past against you."

Trish had been contemplating that fact for four days now. She wanted to let go of the condemnation she felt. She wanted to live free. She wanted to dated Henry.

"I know he wouldn't, but it's hard to let go of the guilt."

"I can't imagine how hard that must be, but I do know how much Cari has struggled since Braydon. I'll pray for you when I pray for her, okay?"

"Yeah, I'd like that."

"As I tell Cari, God can get you through this, but if there is anything I can do – even if it is just to be a shoulder to cry on or an ear to listen – please let me know. You are loved."

Trish blinked. "What is it with you Bennett relations and your need to make me teary by telling me that there are people who love me despite my faults?" She forced a laugh.

Lacey, who was now standing, placed a hand on her shoulder. "I can't speak for Gran, but for me, I know how much I have needed to hear those words at various times in my life. Things can get messy, and it's easy to think you're alone and that no one see or cares for you." She moved to go to the community room but paused before leaving the desk area. "You're not alone."

"Thanks for the reminder." It was one Trish greatly needed. She often felt like an outsider who would never be accepted anywhere – the girl with the scarlet letter.

She picked a book out of the drop at the desk and prepared to scan it back into circulation. While she might be the shunned and shameful misfit in Foster's Arm, she fit here. She fit with the Bennetts and Gran and Lacey and even Tyler, Blake, and Cari.

She put the scanned book on the shelving cart. Would she still fit in if they all knew her story? Lacey hadn't even batted an eyelash at Trish's confession just now. She hadn't clucked her tongue or heaved a deep disappointed sigh. Maybe the others wouldn't either. Maybe they were just as grace-filled as Gran and Lacey.

She pulled out her phone.

Do you want to grab dinner at the diner with me? My treat.

The words of her text stared back at her as she took a deep breath and expelled it slowly hoping that it would help her heart stop beating so quickly. She could do this. She could live as if her past no longer condemned her, couldn't she?

There was only one way to find out. She pressed send and closed her eyes to focus on her breathing until she felt the phone, which she was holding to her chest, vibrate.

Are you asking me out on a date?

Maybe. I don't know. Yes?

That's not a very clear answer, but I'll take it.

Sorry. It's the best I can do right now. So dinner? 6:30?

6:30 works for me. Have you gotten that tire changed yet?

No. I have an appointment for tomorrow to have it done.

Then, I'm driving, and it doesn't matter what argument you try, I'm not listening.

Trish smiled at that. *Rather bossy of you.*

Indeed. *smiley face* Pick you up at 6:00 or 6:15?

6:15. I work until 5:30 and would like to wear something other than work clothes.

"Hey." Ava stood at the desk. "Can I book a computer?"

"Sure, but I have to tell you that tomorrow, Gran plans to come to the library for a few minutes, so if you're planning to write here tomorrow, I might have to give you the computer in the opposite corner."

"As long as it is a corner, and I can see what is happening in the library, I'm good."

"Two hours?"

"Unless you can slip me an extra half-hour?"

Trish laughed. "I can't put you down for more than two, but if no one else is booked – and no one is right now – you can keep working." She plugged in the info that the computer reservation system required. "Are you writing anything interesting?"

"I hope I am," Ava replied. "You looked happy to read whatever message you got on your phone." There was a question in her eyes even if there wasn't one in her tone. "I'll tell you what I'm writing if you tell me what made you look so happy." Eddie crossed from one side of the library to the other, and Ava's eyes followed him.

"A date – sort of – maybe," Trish replied.

"Ooh, do tell," Ava's attention turned back to Trish. "I'm in the middle of writing a romance novel," she whispered that part and looked warily around her. "Clean romance," she added as if she was embarrassed.

"I love a good, sweet romance," Trish assured her. "Eddie's not so fond of them."

Ava's face scrunched. "Seriously? I mean he's a guy, so it might not be his sort of thing, but, I don't know. He strikes me as someone who could enjoy a romance." She shrugged. "Or maybe that's just wishful thinking. Back to you. Is this maybe date with a guy as cute as Eddie?"

Trish rose from her place at the desk. "Let me walk you to the computer room." She put the back-in-fifteen-minutes sign on the desk. "I have pictures."

"I like pictures," Ava said.

Trish opened her phone.

Looking forward to it. See you at 6:15.

She smiled and typed *Me, too.* And the amazing thing was that she was. She really was looking forward to having dinner with Henry. She flipped to her photo gallery.

"This is Eddie's twin, Freddie."

"Eddie and Freddie?" Ava asked with a chuckle.

"Yeah, seems a little harsh of their mom to do that to them, but then, she named them after Austen characters, so she only had so many heroes to choose from."

"She named them after Austen characters?" Ava's expression was as shocked as her tone.

"She did, which means Eddie is Edmund Bertram," Trish continued, "and Freddie is Frederick Wentworth."

Ava leaned closer to Trish as if what she was going to say was not something she would share with just anyone. "I kind of like that, being a writer and all."

Trish smiled. Ava was fun. "This is Brandon, after the colonel."

"Phew! Handsome or what?"

"Right?" Trish flipped to a picture of Lacey and Will at their wedding. "This is Will, who is named for Mr. Darcy."

"Hey, I know her. She works here, right?"

"Yep, she's in the room with all the kids today."

"Did they just get married?"

Trish nodded. "On Jane Austen's birthday, and then he took her to Bath for their honeymoon. Lacey loves all things Jane, though not quite as much as Will's mom does."

"Okay, so we have *Mansfield Park*, *Persuasion*, *Sense and Sensibility*, and *Pride and Prejudice*. Are those Mrs. Bennett's favourite novels? Is that why she picked those names? Doesn't she like *Emma* or *Northanger Abbey*?"

"Oh, we're not done yet. Mrs. Bennett has five sons."

Ava grabbed Trish's arm. "Oh, too funny. Five sons and the last name of Bennett. That would make a terrific fanfiction."

Trish laughed. "You seem to really like Jane Austen, too."

"Oh, I do. Like more than a rational human should but maybe less than someone who names her kids after char-

acters – though I'm not promising I wouldn't do that."
Ava laughed. "I've even written Jane Austen fanfiction."
She put her bag down next to the computer she was going
to use and pulled out her phone and tapped it a few times.
"See this book?" She showed Trish a book that was in
the library's ebook system. "That's mine, but don't tell
anyone. Some people give me funny looks when they find
out."

"We have one of your books? That's so cool."

"You have more than one, actually, but I'll keep that
secret for now." She laughed again and put her phone back
in her bag. "I want to see the other Bennett brother."

Trish flicked to the selfie she had taken of her and Henry
last night. "This is Henry."

"Ooooh, I can see why you were smiling if this is the guy
you're going on a date with. Please, tell me it is. I want to
live vicariously through you."

Trish laughed. "I like you. I think we could get along
quite well, and, yes, this is who I'm going to dinner with
tonight." She studied Henry's smile that lit his face in the
picture. She sighed, and Ava sighed right along with her.

"He's delicious, but..." her eyes flicked to the main part
of the library. "There's something about Eddie."

"Yeah, I know what you mean. I feel that way about
Henry." She flipped one more photo.

"Poor Mr. Knightley got dissed, huh?"

"Only because baby number six was a girl named
Emma." Trish showed her a picture of Emma and Cari.
"The girl with the pink hair is Lacey's sister, Cari."

"Wow, they're both pretty. Are either of them dating?"

"Nope."

"Well, then, it's you who will have to provide me with a glimpse into what is possible for some." She pulled her notebook from her bag and wiggled the computer mouse to get the computer to wake up. "Hey, if you happen to hear of an editor who is willing to read romance, let me know. My editor's mother fell and broke her ankle so she's cutting back on her hours, and I'd like to have a back up for when her schedule is too full."

"Sure, I'll let you know, but right now, the only person I know personally who does editing is Eddie, but he doesn't read romance, and he's a bit of a Jane Austen purist so I'm going to guess fanfiction would fly like a lead balloon with him. He can be a little snobbish about his reading preferences."

"That's too bad. I'd love to have a reason to chat with him." She waggled her eyebrows. "I guess I'll just have to settle for staring longingly at him when I'm avoiding my work." She took a seat. "Hey, good luck with that date tonight. I hope it goes well."

"Thanks." Trish turned her phone towards Ava. "And look what I plan to read afterward."

Ava covered her face. "See, I shouldn't tell people about my books. It makes me so nervous."

"The description sounded intriguing, so relax. I'll only tell you good things."

"No, don't do that. Tell me the truth. If you hate it, say so, just do it gently."

"Will do." Trish turned to go back to the front desk and had almost left the computer room before she turned back. "The Hatfield Falls Christian Church has singles nights once a month with a couple of other churches. If you want, I can get the details for the one in March for you."

"Oh, that'd be awesome! Our church is kind of to-itself a lot, but hey, I'm all in on spending time with some other non-married folks."

"Great. I'll see if I can find out anything tonight and let you know tomorrow."

Trish couldn't keep from smiling as she made her way back to the front desk. She had a new-to-her author to read, a possible new friend, and she'd just invited someone to a church event for the first time in her life.

Hey, guess what I just did? She put the back-in-fifteen sign away and pulled two books out of the bin to be checked in.

Put a book on a shelf?

She shook her head and chuckled softly at Henry's reply.

Nope. I invited someone to come to the next singles night.

Guy or girl?

Girl. Relax. I'm not interested in anyone but you.

Cool, and I know that's not easy for you to say. So, while I will gloat about it privately, I'll leave it at that and not push. But you know I'd like to, right?

Oh, she knew exactly where he wanted this relationship to go, and if she was honest with herself, she wanted the very same thing. And that terrified her. So, after she sent, *Sure do,* to Henry, she typed out another message.

Asked Henry to go to dinner with me. I can do this, right? I can overcome my past, can't I?

Oh, my dear girl, you most certainly can.

Trish drew and released a breath at the reply and was just typing thanks when a second text popped up on her screen.

I want details tomorrow. XO Gran

She deleted the thanks and wrote instead, *Love you too. T-*

She could do this. If God loved her even half as much as she felt loved by Gran, then, she could do this.

"God," she prayed silently as she scanned a book, "I know we haven't talked much lately, but I'd like to come back to you if you'll have me. Thank you for Gran and Lacey and Henry, and please, please, help me to forgive myself so I can love Henry as I want to do."

Chapter 16

COAT. KEYS. WALLET. HENRY patted his back pocket. Nope, no wallet. He hadn't felt this nervous about going out since... well, ever. He grabbed his wallet off the kitchen island.

"Where are you going? Isn't it your night to cook?" Fred, who had just showered off the grime from work, came up the stairs as Henry was putting his wallet in his pocket.

"I've got a date." Henry couldn't keep from grinning as he said that. "I've left money for Chinese food. Let me know if it comes to more than I left, and I'll pay back whoever paid the extra."

"A date? With Trish?"

Henry nodded. "She asked me to join her for dinner at the diner." He still couldn't believe she had done that. Never in a million years would he have expected her to ask him out. He had thought it would still be months before she would be favourable to going on a date with him. Of course, he wasn't going to complain about the timeline being shifted forward. Oh, no, he was more than pleased to have gotten her text today.

"Cool. Did you get her any flowers? Girls like flowers."

"I don't want to scare her off." He had actually thought of getting her a single flower, but then, before he had gotten to *Blooms and Blossoms* he had decided that might be pushing his good luck too far.

"I suppose I can see your point." Fred flipped over the menu for the Chinese place they always ordered from, took out his phone, and began typing. "I'll see what Eddie and Brandon want and order it so it can be here when they get home, and so I don't starve." He feigned a look of displeasure for Henry who laughed.

"There's plenty of other food in the kitchen." He moved toward the entryway.

"How long do you think it'll be before Eddie and I need to find a new place to live?" Fred's tone was teasing.

"It's one date, man. I think we can figure out future living arrangements later."

"But good apartments can be hard to find."

Had his younger brother really just pouted? He shook his head. "Call Will and talk to him about how long it will take. I've got to go." His plan to drive around to warm up his car before picking up Trish was quickly collapsing.

"Think Trish would be okay with us living in the basement?" Fred called after Henry as he ducked out the door.

"I'll ask her – but not tonight." Henry closed the door on Fred's laughter. Brothers could be such a bother.

"Fred says you have a date," Brandon said as he got out of his vehicle. "I'm surprised Trish said yes so soon."

"She didn't say yes," Henry opened the door to his car. "She did the asking. I did the saying yes." Like he was going to answer any other way.

"Good for her." Brandon's smile was broad, and his voice sounded just like it did when Emma did something that made him proud. In that moment, Henry knew the truth about Brandon and Trish's relationship, and he saw his jealousy for the foolishness that it was.

"You never were interested in her as more than a friend or sister, were you?"

Brandon shook his head. "I tried to tell you that."

"Guess I should have listened." But it had been hard to not think that Brandon and Trish would become more than friends from the way they were so comfortable around each other.

"Guess you should have, but I can understand your being jealous of me." He laughed. "Seriously, I hope it goes well tonight. Don't hurt her."

"I wouldn't. You know that."

"Yeah, I do, but Trevor isn't here, and it felt like something that had to be said. Like it's part of the regulations for starting to date someone like Trish." He shrugged and then, sighed. "I'll pray she doesn't hurt you."

Henry's breath puffed out in front of him on the frigid air of an early February evening. "Thanks." He knew it was a possibility. A very great and real possibility. Trish could go out with him this once, and then, go right back to being too scared of him to do more than say hi in passing. As he slipped behind the wheel and started the car, he said his own prayer for protection both for his own heart and hers.

"I'm just about ready." Trish greeted him at her door with a nervous smile and with one boot on a foot and the other in her hand.

"You look great, not that that's anything out of the ordinary."

She gave him a skeptical look as she held his arm to steady herself while she wiggled her foot into her boot.

"I'm not offering empty flattery," he assured her. "I'll only ever be honest with you, Trish."

She gave the back of her boot a tug and then, stamped her foot a couple of times.

"I find you cute," he continued, "no matter what you're wearing. Even if it's those fluffy green slippers and that striped bathrobe with your hair up and a mask on like that time when I saw you at Lacey's house back in the fall."

Trish laughed. "In that case, I don't know why I tried on three different sweaters. I could have just thrown on my sweatpants and hoodie."

"You could have," Henry agreed. "However, that blue sweater looks great with your jeans."

"Jeans aren't too casual, are they?" She stuck one arm into her coat, and Henry reached around to help her with the other sleeve.

"Not at all. It's the diner, not a five-star restaurant." He stood as close to her now as he had in his kitchen that night she had come over for pizza. And just like on that night, he didn't want to move away. He really wanted to pull her close and kiss her. "You look great. Truly."

"You look good, too." She pulled in a deep breath. "You smell even better."

Henry chuckled as her eyes grew wide as if she had spoken something that was supposed to have remained a thought. "Finally." With some effort, he managed to step away from her and motion to the door.

"Finally what?" she asked as she exited the apartment.

"Finally, I get to be on the receiving end of some flirting. I was beginning to think I might not be as attractive as my brothers or something."

"Am I that bad?"

"Bad?" Henry's heart beat at a panicked pace. He hadn't just said something that would send her scurrying again, had he?

"Yeah, bad. I mean Lacey did mention that I tend to flirt too much with Eddie, and I have been trying not to." She stopped moving and now, stood between the open passenger side door and the car, looking at him with wide eyes as if something had just shocked her completely. "Actually," she said slowly, "I don't think I have flirted with Eddie in... well... I think, since before Christmas."

"Why's that?" he asked as she got into the car. Boy, she looked good there. It was as if it was where she belonged – riding shotgun next to him.

"It's probably your fault," she said with a teasing smile before tugging the door shut.

Henry hurried around to his side and climbed in quickly. "How is it my fault?"

"You look really good in a tailcoat."

"What?" He looked over his shoulder as he backed out of her driveway.

"At Will's wedding. I mean, all of you looked good, but..." she shrugged. "I can't explain it. You just looked better."

Whether it made sense or not, he was okay with that explanation. "So, you stopped flirting with Eddie because I look good in a tailcoat?"

"Yes, and no."

"That requires explaining."

The car was silent for what felt like an hour but was realistically probably only a minute.

"You're real."

Ah, New Year's Eve. He'd probably have to thank Brandon for that. Not that he wanted to, but Brandon had been right about what Trish needed to see from him.

"You're not perfect, and you don't pretend to be anything more or less than you are," she continued. "My last boyfriend was a pretender."

That was the first time she had brought up her previous boyfriend. From the way Trish had hidden from him so often, he had long suspected that the boyfriend was a key to whatever troubled her – he had to be why she never planned to marry. Her parents and former church also played a role in this somehow. He knew that from the small comments she had made about each. However, he just had a hunch that the boyfriend was the bedrock on which the rest was built.

"You can tell me about him," Henry offered. "I don't mind. In fact, it might help me understand you better." He glanced across the car at her. She was looking at her clasped hands in her lap. He was right. That boyfriend was the root of Trish's pain.

"I promised myself I would tell you about him tonight."

"You did?"

She nodded and looked at him. "It's only fair that you know all about me so that you can decide if you want to go out with me again or not." She turned in her seat, so she was looking more fully at him. "I had hoped to tell you this after we ate, but it might be better if I get it over with now."

Since they were driving past the church, Henry turned into the parking lot. This seemed like a conversation that they should have face to face and not while he was driving.

"I want to give you my full attention," he explained when she shot him a questioning look. "If whatever you want to share with me has you so on edge that eating while knowing you have to share it makes you uncomfortable, I want to be able to hold your hand if needed. I can't do that while driving."

"I suppose it will also make it easier for us to not go through with the date if you want."

Henry grabbed one of her gloved hands. "That's not why I stopped here."

She shook her head. "I know it's not why you stopped, but I want you to know that if you find what I tell you to be too much, I'll understand if you just take me home, and we don't go to the diner."

His brow furrowed. "There's not much I can think of that would make me want to walk away from you, Trish."

"My former boyfriend was married."

Henry blinked. "Married?"

She nodded. "I didn't know he was, but he was." She turned her eyes away from him as if looking at him while talking was too difficult and began to share a tale of romantic dates, pretty gifts, and broken promises. The telling of it had to be hard, for listening silently was not easy.

"How could he do that?" Henry said when Trish had finished telling him about going ring shopping and how he – Michael, the scumbag – had never called or came back after that date.

"It's worse." She tried to pull her hand away from him, but he refused to let go. "I thought Michael and I were going to get married, so I agreed to..." She paused.

"You slept with him?"

She nodded, and he saw a tear slip down her cheek.

"I'm not a virgin either, remember?"

Again, she nodded. "I got pregnant," she whispered.

Everything stood still for a moment as Henry processed that. This was why she had asked him if the girl he had slept with got pregnant or not. So many things about Trish were beginning to make a lot of sense. "What happened to the baby?"

"I lost it." She shook her head as if she did not want to remember that part.

"I'm sorry." He gave her hand a squeeze before releasing it so he could hand her the pack of tissues his mom had insisted he needed to have in his car. He'd have to thank her for being demanding at some point.

Trish looked up at him with teary eyes. "That's it? You're sorry?"

"What else am I supposed to say? I can see that losing your baby was devastating to you. I'm sorry it was."

She dried her tears and blew her nose. "You don't condemn me?"

He shook his head. "I could've been a father after that night in the boathouse. We all make choices that are less than great. I'm sorry your decision ended in so much pain."

She sank back in her seat and shook her head. "I can't... you and Gran..." She shook her head. "Do you know what my parents did when they found out about it?"

"I could guess, but no, I don't know for sure."

"So, I had just found out that I was pregnant, and that my boyfriend, who had promised to buy that engagement ring as soon as he landed the next big account, was a married man – a married man! Oh, I was so stupid." She shook her head again.

"You were not stupid. You were deceived."

"I should have suspected something. He acted really off sometimes." She blew out a breath. "When I finally decided to track him down and showed up at his church, I found out that his wife had just died. I guess she was sick and had been for some time, which meant that when he should have been with her and his children, he had been with me. I often wonder if she knew about me or suspected there was someone. It must have caused her so much heartache."

Henry cursed the invention of center consoles, for he longed to do more than hold her hand. He now understood her comments about not feeling like she deserved anything good in her life. He understood better than anyone else likely could, for he had felt the same way after Jake died.

"I lost the baby two weeks after that."

"Is that when your parents found out?"

She nodded. "And shortly after that is when the pastor of our church was told about my going to Michael's church and announcing myself as his girlfriend. Someone there had heard me and discovered who I was and where I lived and went to church. I don't know who she was to Michael or his wife, but I can only imagine she was close to them since she went to such lengths to humiliate me."

"By telling your pastor?"

"My pastor was not like your father. The last time I went to Sunday school at my old church, I was surprised to find myself the object of his lesson on church discipline." She wiped her eyes. "In front of all the adults and teens in the church, my parents told him about the baby when he asked if I had done more than date a married man. I tried to tell them that I didn't know he was married and that we were engaged when we had sex." She shook her head.

"He wouldn't listen." He couldn't imagine how horrible that all would have been.

"None of them listened. I was a fallen woman who needed to pay for my sins." Her voice was filled with anger. "I used some language that was not at all God-honouring and walked out of the meeting. My parents were counseled to give me a couple of weeks before they insisted that I go back to church. I refused, and they told me that I was no longer welcome in their home. I left that night. It was Christmas Eve."

Henry's brow furrowed, and he shook his head. He simply could not fathom how people who claimed to be Christian, let alone parents, could be so heartless.

"Oh, Trish, sorry is too shallow a word for how it makes me feel to know you were treated like that." He took a tissue from the pack she held. "They were wrong. So very wrong to do that to you." He wiped at the tears that had gathered in his own eyes. Then, he placed a hand gently on her cheek. "No one should be treated that way." His thumb stroked her cheek. "Do you still want to go to the diner?"

"Do you?"

"I want to do whatever you want. I won't press you to date me if you don't want to, but I don't plan to stop trying to convince you that you should date – and maybe even marry – me."

A deep crease formed between her eyes, and she opened her mouth to speak but shut it again as if she did not know what to say.

"I'm pretty sure I'm in love with you. What happened in your past is not going to change that fact."

"But I'm used, broken."

"So am I, but God and Brandon can both make beautiful things out of broken stuff."

She chuckled softly at that.

"Don't tell Brandon I compared him to God. He'll never let me forget it."

"How can you love me? You barely know me."

"I wish I could give you a good answer to that, but I can't. I just love you, and I do know some things about you. You don't like onions. You love ginger snaps, which I hope includes me." He gave her one of his best smiles and got another chuckle just as he had intended to do. "You love my grandmother, and she loves you. You like to jog, but not in the winter because of ice. You're into reading books, but I don't know what kind. You dislike action movies. Let's see... what else do I know?"

"Those are not things that inspire love."

"Why not?"

She looked at him as if he was mad. "They just don't."

"I know you truly want to walk with God and do what is right."

She shook her head. "How do you know that?"

"Because of what you went through and the fact that you still let Gran and I talk about God, and you ask things like *how do I learn to forgive myself.*" He shrugged. "Remember, I've been in a similar spot as far as messing things up goes. At least, you didn't know you were walking down a dangerous path when you first accepted a date with Michael. I, on the other hand, threw myself into sin with gusto and knew that the path I had chosen was wrong."

"You still don't know much about me," she protested somewhat weakly.

"Then, let me take you to the diner, and you can tell me all about you over a hot turkey sandwich, a root beer, and a slice of lemon pie."

"You're really not going to walk away?"

He framed her face with his hands and pulled her towards him so he could kiss her forehead. "Never." He looked into her eyes and considered kissing her lips, but then, deciding it was too soon for that, he gave her forehead one more kiss before removing his hands from her face and turning to start the car. "I'll take the long way to the diner. That should give your eyes some time to clear, okay?"

She smiled and nodded. "But I don't like lemon pie."

"Ah, see! Already I'm learning more to love about you."

"How does my not liking lemon pie make me more lovable?" She was looking at him again as if he was missing a few connections in his brain.

"Because I love lemon pie, and since you don't, that leaves more of it for me."

She rolled her eyes and shook her head at his foolishness as he pulled out of the church parking lot.

"Thank you," she said when they had gone a distance down the road.

"For what?"

"Well, for a couple of things, I guess. First, for not walking away, and second, for not saying 'because you're hot' when I asked you how you could love me."

"Let me guess, that's what Scumbag said when you asked him why he loved you?"

"You got it." She glanced at him and smiled. "And that's a pretty great name for him."

"It's better than he deserves," Henry muttered.

"I totally agree."

"But just so we're clear here, while hot is not a word I would use for you because it's not a word I tend to use, I most certainly find you attractive, as well as enticing, bewitching, enchanting, and beautiful – all of that and likely more words that Eddie would know off the top of his head but would take me longer to think of."

Her hand slipped around his elbow where it rested on the center console and settled into the crook of his arm. It fit there perfectly, and he wondered if any other fellow had ever felt so blessed as he did to be trusted so completely by such a precious lady as the one who had just laid out before him her deepest, most painful secret.

Chapter 17

"Why didn't I know you had a date with Henry?" Lacey demanded before Trish could even say hi to her the next day at the library.

Trish looked from Lacey to Edmund who was just hanging up his coat in the staff area.

"I didn't tell her," he said.

"What's this about a date?" Jenna, another one of Trish's co-workers, asked as she closed the door to her locker. "I go away to have a baby and come back to news that Eddie's oldest brother is married, and now you have actually gone on a date? I thought you'd sworn off men?"

"Welcome back, Jenna." Trish gave her a hug. "How's the little bug today? Was it hard leaving him at daycare?"

"Oh, not for him. Me, on the other hand..." She emptied a handful of tissues from her pocket into the trash can and laughed. "Now, tell me what persuaded you to give guys another try?"

"My brother," Eddie answered.

"Oh! A date with Henry – as in handsome Bennett brother number three?"

"That's the one," Lacey answered this time. "Why didn't I know you were going on a date with him?"

"How did you know I had gone out with him?" Trish took her time putting her lunch in her locker.

"That would be Fred's fault," Eddie answered. "He told everyone – Brandon, me, Will, Mom, Gran, Dad, and who knows who else."

Everyone? Trish rested a hand on her heart. "Okay, now, I get why Will kept your relationship a secret," she said to Lacey.

Lacey simply glared at her in reply.

"I didn't know if the date was going to work or not," she explained.

"How could it not work?"

That was a question Trish did *not* want to answer. "No relationship is guaranteed."

"But it's Henry. He's crazy about you, and I happen to know you're not indifferent to him."

"That still doesn't mean things will work out."

"I say it's good to be cautious," Jenna agreed. "Especially when you've been hurt enough to declare dating off limits."

"Who said I was hurt before?"

"No one, but a cute girl like you who appreciates the handsome things in life doesn't give up dating because she finds the thought repulsive."

"Okay, you've got me there, I suppose." And she hoped that would put an end to this discussion.

"It's five to ten. Time to get things ready and unlock the library." Edmund held the door to the staff room open for them. "Do you remember the opening procedure?" he asked Jenna.

"I think I do. I'll get the books from the after-hours drop and start scanning them in."

"I'll make sure the chairs are off the tables," Trish said. At night, the cleaners always put the chairs up to vacuum.

"And I'll start on the hold requests," Lacey said as she took Trish's arm.

It seemed slipping away into the busyness of the morning was not going to be an option.

"Did you have a good time with Henry?"

"I did." Henry had been just as he always was – adorable, sweet, and caring. Her phone vibrated.

Good morning, beautiful. It read.

Back at you, handsome. She typed in reply.

"Was it from Henry?" Lacey asked eagerly.

"Yes. He said good morning."

"Aw."

Trish gave Lacey a playful shove. "Don't start. No sappy stuff. This still might not work out. Go start your hold requests."

"I want date details at some point." She stood looking at Trish for a moment longer before grabbing her in a tight embrace. "I'm just so happy for you."

"I'm rather happy for myself, too," Trish admitted. The trouble was that she still felt kind of guilty about being happy. Walking in grace – that area free from condemnation – wasn't easy. "We went to the diner and talked. It wasn't all that eventful. It was just nice, and I like him more now that I did before."

"Any other dates planned?"

"I'm going to meet him and Tyler and Blake at the diner tomorrow before church, but we've got nothing planned besides that." She began putting down chairs in the social area. She would get the computer room next.

"Is that a date?"

Trish shrugged. "Maybe? But..." She stood with her hands resting on the back of the chair she had just put next to the table. "Honestly, I don't care if it's a date or not. I'm just happy to spend time with him and be included in his life."

Lacey smiled. "I know just what you mean. All those weeks when Will and I were secretly seeing each other, I looked forward to any time we were together and longed for the day when I could be a greater and non-secret part of his life. I really am happy for you," she added before going to the front desk.

Trish finished putting down all the chairs in the social area and then moved to the computer room. She heard the front door open and close. A few kids' voices filtered back to where she was. Maybe one day, she'd get to bring her kids to the library on a Saturday morning. The thought made her smile.

"Thank you, God," she whispered. She had thought her chance of ever being a mother had been taken from her when her baby died, but if she married Henry, that deep desire might one day be fulfilled. She sat down on the chair she had just put down and thought about Henry as a father and husband until her phone vibrated, interrupting her rumination.

Mom wants to know if you would like to join me for Sunday dinner at her place. Fred told her about our date.

Trish sighed. Yep, she could really understand Will's desire to date in secret.

Sure. I think I can do that. Can I bring anything?

Just you. XO

"The chairs won't put themselves down," Edmund said in a teasing tone as he poked his head into the computer room.

Trish rose from where she was sitting.

"Want to watch a movie at our place tonight?" Edmund asked. "Fred's making nachos and chili."

"Just me and the four of you?"

"There might be a few others. Maybe Emma and Cari and Will and Lacey." He leaned against the front computer desk. "Fred promises not to pick an action movie. He's trying to find an acceptable comedy."

"Sure. It sounds like fun."

Eddie pushed off the desk. "By the way, I'm glad you're dating my brother."

"You are?"

"Yep. You seem right for each other, and I haven't seen him quite so happy in a long time."

"Thanks. I honestly haven't been this happy in years."

"Don't hurt him."

Trish blinked. "I don't plan to hurt him."

"I didn't think you did, but he really went through a dark time after..." He shrugged instead of finishing his thought.

"After Jake?"

Edmund nodded. "He didn't say much, but we could tell he was struggling. It's probably what makes him so good at helping others now. Dad always says that trials come into our lives for reasons. Sometimes they are the result of poor life choices – Henry's was that way – but sometimes, they are also of God's design to help us grow. Either way, they teach us things that help us become better equipped to share God's love and minister to others." Again, he shrugged as if he was somewhat uncomfortable talking about things like this with her – or maybe it was that he was uncomfortable about talking about these things with anyone. "I got that sermon a few times when I was at college and missing home or wrestling with some project. Thankfully, my trials have been fairly small so far."

"You're lucky. Mine have been kind of big." That was putting it mildly.

"That's too bad, but maybe that means you'll get to do greater things for God because of them." He followed her to the teen computer area.

"Maybe, though I have yet to figure out how what I've gone through can be used to help anyone."

"He'll show you. At least, that's what Dad says." He put a chair down for her. "I'll let Fred know that you'll come tonight, and I have a couple of books to repair while manning the information desk, so I'll talk to you later." And with a wave he was gone.

Trish put down the three remaining chairs and contemplated the most serious conversation that she and Eddie had ever had. They talked about books and normal, everyday stuff, but this was the first time that they had ever talked about God and life. It was also the first time she had heard him talk so lovingly about any of his brothers. She had heard him talk that way about his mom and grandmother but not his brothers.

She pulled out her phone.

Thanks for talking to me about God that day in the parking lot. You didn't know me, but you cared enough to ask me about God.

Michael had never once asked her anything about her relationship with God. He had asked if she went to church and which church it was, but he never even prayed before they ate on their dates. She shook her head. She hadn't realized at that time just how much she valued someone to talk to about God. She laughed softly to herself. That was likely because at the time, she hadn't valued what she did now.

Seriously? I thought I had blown any chance I had with you by asking you about your relationship with God.

She stared at Henry's reply. From the start he had put God before her. She smiled. She hadn't thought there were guys like that in the world.

You want to come over and watch a movie tonight?

Already am. Eddie invited me, she replied.

But you're dating me, right?

Yes, only you.

Just making sure.

A bit of a commotion caught Trish's attention. Turning toward the ruckus, she saw the best sight she had seen at the library in some time. Brandon was being swatted away from helping Gran with her walker.

"She wouldn't hear of using her chair," he grumbled to Trish when he came to where she was gathering her books to shelve. "But at least she let me help her get from my van to the inside of the library before she started telling me that I could leave."

"She'll be fine. We'll keep a close eye on her if you aren't planning to stay."

"Did things go well last night?"

"They did."

"Good. Henry said the same, but I wanted to make sure you were okay. Not that I thought my brother would do something to hurt you or whatever, but..." He rubbed the back of his neck. "I'd feel the same way if Emma were dating a good friend, know what I mean?"

"I do. I kind of classify you in the same spot as Trevor."

He smiled. "That's exactly where I want to be, and who knows, maybe some day I'll actually be your brother."

"Maybe."

"Yeah? Really? You'd be okay with that?"

"I think I would be, but we've only been on one date."

"Sometimes one date is all that is needed."

"I doubt that." Falling in love in a forever kind of way took time, didn't it?

"No, really. You should ask my dad about him and mom. They dated for a week before he proposed, and he had decided he was going to marry her before he even went out with her on that first date."

At least, now, she knew where Henry got his ability to talk marriage before he had even been on one date with her.

"I still don't know how that can happen," she admitted.

"Me, either," Brandon said. "I thought I was going to marry Zoe after we had been dating for a couple of months, but then..." He spread his hands out as if to indicate that he had nothing.

Trish patted his shoulder. "Your one-date lady is out there somewhere, and no, I doubt her name is Zoe. I still don't see how she could walk away from a guy like you. You're pretty awesome."

"Thanks. You're not half bad yourself, kid."

"She's better than that." Gran had finally made it past the front desk and into the main library. "And I have told Edmund that you will shelve those books as soon as I hear about your date."

"Good luck," Brandon said with a laugh. "She hasn't been out enough. Her social skills are slipping."

"Oh, hush! My social skills are just fine," Gran retorted before laughing. "Actually, I'm not sure they were ever terribly good."

"I'll be back in an hour."

"I'll be at my computer." She turned to Trish as Brandon walked away. "He refuses to take me to his studio. He says one place per outing is all I get to visit until he hears from my doctor or physio that I can do more than that." She shook her head. "I never would have pegged him as a coddler, but it seems he is."

"He loves you, and none of us want you to overdo things and hurt yourself."

"Get over here and give me a hug, and then, you can push that cart to the computer room so you can tell me if Henry treated you well."

"Would you expect him to treat me poorly?" Trish asked as she gave Gran the hug she demanded.

"No, I wouldn't, but he's Henry and not infallible." She began walking toward the computer room. "Where did you go?"

"Just to the diner. Their hot turkey sandwich is delicious. Henry insisted I would like it, and he was right. They make real gravy. It's not that horrible, canned stuff some places use. And the apple pie is divine."

"Did Henry have lemon pie?"

"He did."

"It's his favourite."

"He said it was. I'm glad someone likes it."

"You don't?"

"Nope. Pudding-like filling and pie crust." She shuddered, and Gran laughed.

"Do you like pudding by itself?"

"I do. It's just the combination of pudding and pie crust that I find unpleasant. I suppose the meringue on top doesn't help since I'm not a fan of that either."

Trish parked her shelving cart at the front of the computer room and then, hovered behind Gran to make sure she got to her computer and seated safely.

"You're pretty good at the coddling thing, too." She gave Trish a pointed look.

"It's your first time here, and I don't want you to get hurt and not be able to come back for a while. We've missed you."

Gran smiled at that. "I've missed being here."

Trish pulled a chair over to sit next to Gran. "I told him."

Gran looked at her in surprise. "Everything?"

Trish nodded. "I didn't want to start a relationship without everything being perfectly honest between us." She looked toward the main library. "I'm going to tell Lacey soon. I can't keep hiding."

"It sounds like you're finally breaking free."

"It feels like I am. It's as if each time I tell my story, I feel less bound by it."

"The enemy likes to use shame and guilt to keep us from being used as fully by God as we could be. Henry learned that, mostly, when he was coming back to God. However, I think he's learning that fully with you."

"What do you mean?"

"I heard him and Brandon at Will's place on New Year's Eve, and when I asked him about it, he admitted it was because he thought you'd think less of him." She patted Trish's hand. "But you didn't, did you?"

"No, I appreciated that he didn't hide anything from me, and he hasn't that I know of."

"He won't. Even when it's hard. He's done his share of hiding things in the past, and like you, he's not interested in living any way other than honestly."

"I really love him, Gran. Like more than I did the other day at your apartment."

"I'm happy to hear that. That's how the way it should be. And, I'm still praying."

"Good."

Gran chuckled. "You weren't so happy to have me praying for you to marry my grandson before my surgery."

"That was because I didn't think it was possible then, but I'm learning that God isn't exactly who I thought He was. He has given me you and Henry and Brandon and Lacey..." She felt completely overwhelmed by the goodness God had allowed in her life even after she had messed things up so badly by dating Michael. "His love is rather overwhelming."

"Oh, it is wonderfully overwhelming."

"I better go shelve those books. I'm only here until two today. I'll send you some pictures from Brandon's studio. He's going to teach me how to do the flowers between glass thing like he made from Lacey's bouquet. I'd like a couple to hang in my apartment's bathroom, and he mentioned trying flowers in resin to see if we could make a soap dish or a plate for a candle."

"That sounds like a lot of fun. Next week, you and Henry need to come bake cookies with me. My physiotherapist said I could start baking with assistance."

"I'll see which day we both have time off, and we'll be there."

"Trish," Gran called before she could get all the way to her cart of books.

"Yes?"

"I love you, my dear girl, and I'm so very proud of how brave you were to ask Henry out and tell him about... well, you know."

"Don't make me cry!" Trish smiled as she blinked away the tears that sprang to her eyes. "I love you, too." She turned to her cart and pulled it out from next to the wall. She gave one last glance over her shoulder to see Gran happily typing away on her computer's keyboard before heading off to the 600s section of the library to put away the cookbooks that lined the top shelf of her cart.

Chapter 18

"Did you get those cookies baked?" Will asked as he came to stand next to Henry in the church foyer between Sunday school and morning service.

"Yep, yesterday afternoon. It was nice to see Gran in her element again." Henry took a sip from his coffee cup and tapped open the browser on his phone with the thumb of his hand that wasn't holding his coffee.

"I've been looking at these." He tilted his screen towards Will. "No one else knows so don't say anything. What do you think? They aren't traditional, but they kind of look like Trish, don't you think?"

Will took the phone and scrolled through the selection of engagement rings that were not solely diamonds. "These are beautiful, but you've only gone out a few times. How long has it been since she asked you out? A week?"

"A week and a day, and I know. But that's just it – I know." Trish was *the* person for him. He wanted to continue to grow in grace along side her. He wanted to be allowed to cherish and protect her forever – or until God called him heaven. "Do you think they look like her?"

Will shrugged. "I think so, but Brandon would know better."

"I don't want to ask him."

Will chuckled. "Why? I thought the jealousy thing was over."

"It is. I don't know. I just don't want to ask him. I trust you more to keep my secret and not throw me under a bus while trying to help me." Like he had at Will's place on New Year's Eve.

"But the truth is, he helped you." Will gave Henry a pointed look as he handed the phone back to him.

Henry slipped his phone back in his pocket. "I'll consider it." Even if he didn't want to, he had to. Will was right far too often to not consider it.

"When?" Will asked.

Henry shrugged. "I'm not sure, but soon. I want her to know she's loved forever."

Will's lips twitched. "So, not today in the church foyer?"

Henry chuckled. "No. I don't plan to copy you."

"It worked." Will smiled at his wife as she and Trish joined them. "Is Gran settled?"

"As settled as we can convince her to be," Lacey replied.

"She's doing really well," Trish added. "I thought she'd be a bit slower moving today since she spent so much time helping us in the kitchen yesterday. By the way, we have a tin of ginger snaps for today's teatime."

"Oh, Mom will love that," Will said.

"What will Mom love?" Brandon rubbed his hands together and blew into them. "It's still cold out there." He had just come in from parking his van after delivering Gran to Trish and Lacey at the church door.

"The ginger snaps Trish and I made at Gran's yesterday."

"Oh, yes, the cookies." He rolled his eyes. "I heard *all* about them this morning. From the way Gran was carrying on, Emma might want to think about hiring you, Henry, when she and Cari need baking staff."

"That's not going to happen," Henry replied with a laugh. "However, I think I can add a skill to my repertoire of culinary excellence. I'm up to expert pizza maker and better-than-most cookie maker."

"While I'm pleased to hear that, I don't think Freddie or Eddie want to eat cookies for supper."

"But, they might want to eat them *with* supper," Trish suggested as she slipped her hand into Henry's. "Did you finish getting your video edited?" she asked his brother.

Brandon nodded. "I did. Thanks for your help with staining those frames so I could get started on that the other day. Speaking of that, before I could leave to go get Gran at the end of Sunday school, I ran into Mrs. Martin. She made a point to pull me aside in an empty hallway and whisper that it might be best if you and I weren't alone so often in my studio. After all, I live upstairs now, and temptation happens." He rolled his eyes and shook his head. "I assured her that you were merely a friend, whom I hoped would one day be my sister, but she said that gossips don't care about details like that, and she'd feel dreadful if rumours circulated and she hadn't, at least, cautioned me."

Henry watched Trish carefully to see how this information sat with her. As expected, he saw her chin lift as she drew in a breath.

"How did Mrs. Martin know that you and Trish were alone at your studio?" he asked.

"Gran showed her pictures of some of my projects when she visited her this week. Trish was in those pictures."

"But we were in a studio with huge glass windows that anyone could look through and see us," Trish protested.

"I agree. It's ridiculous, but she's just trying to be helpful. She's not a vicious gossip. Gran doesn't keep gossips as friends," Brandon assured her.

Trish gave Henry a look that asked if he believed what Brandon said was true or not.

"Yeah, Gran might share news, but she doesn't tell tales." That earned him a small smile.

"Well, I suppose, it's almost time to go in." Trish looked towards the hall where the bathrooms were. "Save me a place, okay?"

"Even if you didn't ask me," Henry assured her.

"You should show Brandon," Will whispered as Henry drained his cup of coffee.

"Fine. Let me toss this in the garbage. Brandon." He tilted his head towards the welcome center where the coffee and tea were kept. "I asked Will his opinion on these, but he thought you would be a better person to ask." He opened the browser on his phone again. "Do any of these look like Trish to you? I don't want to get her something ordinary. I want something as special as she is."

"Wow. You're thinking about this? Already?"

Henry shrugged and stepped away from Brandon to throw his coffee cup in the garbage can.

"These are perfect," Brandon said when Henry rejoined him.

"Yeah? You're sure?"

"Oh, I'm more than sure. This blue topaz one is really close to the colour of the dress she wore in Lacey's wedding, and that shade of blue looked really pretty on her. It set off her hair and eyes perfectly. It's definitely a Trish colour, and I'd be the first to tell you that she likes things that are unique."

"That was my favourite. She wore a blue sweater on our first date." Henry smiled sheepishly at his brother. "I know. I would tease any of you if you were picking a ring based on a sweater your girlfriend wore."

Brandon chuckled. "Yeah, and I might still tease you about it at some point, but not today. I'm happy for both you and her." He expelled a breath. "She's healing. You can both see it and feel it in her."

That was true. Trish smiled more now than she had when Henry had first met her, and it was a smile that didn't just curve her lovely pink lips upward, it was an expression that sparkled in her eyes and danced on her laugh. She no longer seemed to shrink into herself and try to hide in plain sight. Her body language was much more open. However, there was still a hesitancy about her, especially when it came to accepting new people into her circle of friends at church.

The same was not true at the library, but then, she had never been devastatingly hurt by anyone she trusted at the library the way she had been at her former church. It was only natural for her to have some lingering wariness and anxiety.

"These are my brothers," Will said as Henry and Brandon approached him where he was talking to someone who was new to their church. "Brandon and Henry." He motioned to each of them in turn. "This is Michael. He and his family are visiting today on their way to their March break destination. Their hotel recommended our church."

"Is it your first time to Hatfield Falls?" Brandon asked.

"It is. I'm a regional manager at my company, and they just recently reorganized territories, so Hatfield Falls is now part of my substantially larger area. But, at least, with the increased need to travel comes an increase in pay, so it's all good."

"Where do you call home?" Henry asked.

"A little place called Port Lonish."

Realization of who Michael was shot through Henry with all the comfort of a hot poker. "That's near Foster's Arm, isn't it?" Where was Trish? He prayed she was still in the bathroom. He'd do the expected friendly welcoming things, and then, he'd slip away to find her before she found Michael.

"It is. Do you know that place?"

"We have a couple of friends from there," Brandon answered.

"It's not a large place. I might know them."

Oh, he did. Henry was certain he did.

"Trish and Trevor Thompson. They call Hatfield Falls home now."

Henry watched fear flicker in Michael's eyes at Brandon's reply. That confirmed it. This was Trish's ex.

"I need to do something before the service begins. If you'll excuse me." Henry began to move away from his brothers and Michael, but he was no more than a couple of steps away when his phone vibrated.

Looking at it he read, *I can't do this. I thought I could, but I can't. I'm sorry. So very sorry.* Henry froze in his tracks. Trish. Had she seen Michael? Or was it what Mrs. Martin had said to Brandon that was causing her to flee?

"Oh, there you are!"

"I don't have time, Mom." He looked around the foyer and then towards the hall that led to the ladies' room. "I need to find Trish." Panic coursed through his veins. He needed to get to her.

"She left, dear."

"What?"

"We've been looking for you." She indicated the lady next to her.

Why would a stranger be looking for him?

"I had just finished helping Marjorie settle her little ones into junior church when we came upon Trish." She smiled at the lady next to her. "Henry, dear, this is Marjorie. She and her new husband, Michael, and his children are visiting with us today."

"Marjorie." Michael's new wife. Why did he need to know anything about this lady and her stepchildren? He only wanted to know where Trish was. "You said Trish left?"

"She was looking rather pale and said she wasn't feeling well. She asked me to tell you that she needed to leave and would text or call you later."

Henry looked at his phone. How did Trish know Marjorie? "Yeah, she did. Just now. Did you introduce her to

Marjorie?" He handed his phone to his mom and ran a hand through his hair.

"Just briefly. She seemed to be in a hurry to leave."

"She was leaving before you introduced Marjorie?"

"Yes." His mother's brow furrowed in confusion. "Why?" Her eyes turned to the words on the screen of Henry's phone.

Horrid realization engulfed Henry. If Trish hadn't known this was Michael's wife before she decided to leave, then there was only one other reason seeing Marjorie would have sent Trish fleeing.

"Have you been to Foster's Arm?" he asked Marjorie, who grimaced and nodded.

Henry closed his eyes and shook his head. There were so many things going through his mind that he wanted to say. "You told her pastor." He said it softly.

"I was angry," Marjorie said quickly. "My best friend had died. I blamed everyone."

"What are you talking about?" his mother asked as she handed his phone back to him. "And why can't Trish do this? Does she mean you and her?"

"I assume so." Oh, his heart broke for Trish more than it did for himself. "You were angry at everyone, and yet, you married Michael?" The only one who truly deserved everyone's wrath. "I'm sorry. I need to go."

"Henry, what are you talking about?"

"I can't tell you, and I hope no one else does either. It's Trish's story to tell when and if she decides to tell it. Just know that Trish isn't sick. She's hurting." He pressed his lips together as tears gathered in his own eyes. He could only imagine the fear and hurt that was raging in Trish at the moment.

"Tell her I'm sorry," Marjorie begged. "I spread rumours about her," she said to Henry's mom. "I have long regretted what I did. You'll tell her? Please?" Marjorie asked Henry.

Henry nodded. "When I find her. Pray that I do, Mom, and that she'll listen to me."

"Of course, sweetie. I'll take care of the ninety-nine. You go get that one dear lamb."

He gave her cheek a kiss. "I'll do my best." He took off for the door at a run.

"What's chasing you?" Trevor asked as Henry passed him.

Henry stopped. "Michael and his new wife are here."

"Michael? The one that Trish..."

"Yes. That Michael."

"Did Trish see him?"

Henry shook his head. "No, she met his wife."

"I'm a little confused. How would she know some lady she met was Michael's wife?"

"My mom introduced them, but she was leaving before that because Michael's wife isn't just some lady. She's *the* lady. You know, the one who spoke to your former pastor?"

Trevor's eyes grew wide. "No!"

"I'm afraid so. Her name is Marjorie, and she wants me to tell Trish she's sorry." He blew out a breath. Oh, he didn't want to deliver that message. Sorry was such a meaningless word when compared to the grief that Marjorie's actions had caused for Trish.

"Sorry," Trevor scoffed.

"I know, but maybe she truly is. She seemed sincere." He moved towards the door again.

"I'm coming with you."

"There might be a bit of a mess back there with my mom. I said some things to Marjorie that has her asking questions."

"There'll be a bigger mess if I have to talk to either Michael or Marjorie." Trevor held Henry's gaze.

"Fine. Come with me. She's running scared." He and Trevor hurried toward the far door to the parking lot. "There was something said to Brandon about it not being good for him and her to be alone at his studio because of rumours, and then, shortly after that, she sees Marjorie."

Trevor clapped Henry on the shoulder. "We'll find her, and I know you'll convince her to stick around. She loves you, man. I won't let her give that up."

"Thanks. I won't either, and so you know, I plan to marry her. Are we both taking my car?"

"Yep. Just in case I'm needed to drive Trish's car back here or to her place. I just need to get my van before tomorrow."

"I'll make sure you get back to your van." Henry unlocked the doors to his car. "Do you have any idea where to start looking? I was thinking we should start at her house, but I kind of doubt she'll be there."

"It's a good place to start, and the drive over there will give me some time to think about where else she might go."

Chapter 19

Trish fumbled with the key to unlock her apartment. Tears clouded her vision and fear gripped her heart. She didn't want to leave Hatfield Falls. She wanted to stay here with Henry and Gran and Lacey and Will and Brandon and all the others, but how could she stay now that *that* woman knew where she was?

She threw her purse and jacket on the couch and hurried to her room to pack a bag. She'd spend a few days somewhere that wasn't here, trying to figure out her next move.

She stuffed a few sweaters and a couple of pairs of jeans and yoga pants in her bag along with underwear, socks, and bras. She filled a case with the things she needed from her bathroom and tossed that on top before zipping the bag closed.

Shoes! She unzipped her bag and put in her sneakers and a pair of black flats. She'd wear her boots for now.

That was it. That was all she needed. She looked around at what had been her home and safe haven for two years. She would miss it just as much as she would miss everything else about Hatfield Falls. Her eyes fell on the plate of cookies on the counter. She couldn't leave those behind.

She'd take them and a sandwich. Maybe a thermos of juice would be good, too. Eventually, she'd need to eat.

She packed her lunch bag, and then, with it, her travel bag, coat, and purse, she stepped out into the cold and closed the door on what had been. She wasn't sure where she was going as she backed out of the driveway and onto the road. Surely, a destination would come to mind as she drove – well, once, she got gas. This was a good reason to not let her car run so low on fuel. It made her getaway slower, and she knew she didn't have a lot of time.

Her phone buzzed. Trevor. She'd see what he had to say later. Right now, she had to get to the gas station that was furthest from her house and closest to the edge of Hatfield Falls.

Marjorie. That was the name Mrs. Bennett had used when talking to *that* woman, and it would forever be a name Trish despised. In her opinion Marjorie was even more contemptible than Michael, and his name was at the top of the list of names she would never, and she meant never, name anything – not a dog, not a cat, not a fish, not even an outhouse. Every one of those things was too good for a name like Michael.

She opened Trevor's text before she got out to pump gas.

Heard you were sick? Are you at home? I'd like to check on you.

She tapped the steering wheel. What could she tell him that was true and yet would not give away where she was?

No. Getting some air. There, that would do. She put her phone on airplane mode, got out of her car, and began the cold work of filling it. Why couldn't have Michael and his new wife visited on a warm day?

Her hand released the pump lever. His new wife? The words sank into her brain. Marjorie and Michael were married? She squeezed the pump handle again to start the flow of gas into her car.

Hadn't Marjorie, while resting her hand on her little baby bump, said something to Mrs. Bennett about Michael's wife being her best friend? Her lips curled in disgust. She wasn't sure she would want her best friend marrying her husband just – how long had they been married? Eighteen months? Trish was nearly positive that's what had been said while she had struggled to control her emotions and keep from vomiting in the hall of the church. As it was, she needed to toss that bag in the trash before she left the gas station. It was probably for the best that she had forgotten to remove it from the car at her apartment. She'd hate to come back to a place that smelled like puke that had been ripening for three days.

She shuddered as she returned the nozzle to the pump. Then, she grabbed the bag from the passenger's side and threw it in the trash bin under the window washing station before going in to pay for her gas and grab a bottle of water. She should have gotten one of those from home, but her mind was not working as well as it should be.

Back in the car, she rummaged through her bag to get her toothbrush and toothpaste. Then, after using part of the water in the bottle she had bought to clean her teeth, she took a drink of it before starting her car's engine.

Eighteen months. That meant that less than a year after Michael had buried his first wife, he had married his wife's best friend. She put the car in gear as she wondered if Marjorie and Michael had been more than friends while Michael's wife had been alive. He had dated and slept with her, so Trish would not be surprised to learn she was not the only person he was cheating with.

Disgust at having been one of the other women in Michael's life turned Trish's stomach, threatening to cause her to throw up again.

She switched on the radio. She needed to clear her mind of Michael for a few minutes so she could decide if she should head north or south when she reached the highway. Music from a guitar and piano accompanying singing tugged at her heart. She imagined standing next to Henry and being part of the congregational hymn that played on the radio. She should turn to a different station. It would do her no good to listen to Pastor Bennett. It would only make things harder to leave behind.

But she liked his preaching. She truly felt that her soul was being fed each and every Sunday. That was not something she had ever felt in her former church. Oh, she had felt conviction to do better, to try to improve so she could please God and avoid His judgement, and she knew that such thoughts were not altogether bad. She did need to ferret out sin and remove it from her life, but there was more to being a Christian than that. Gran had taught her that.

"Oh, Gran!" Trish cried as she turned onto the highway. "What am I supposed to do?"

Listen to the service, her mind replied, causing her to smile sadly. That was most likely what Gran would say.

"Good morning," Pastor Bennett said. "Today, we are going to begin by looking at the story of a woman in hiding. We find her story in John chapter four."

A woman in hiding? That definitely caught Trish's attention, and she turned the volume up as Pastor Bennett read.

"And Jesus, tired as he was from the journey, sat down by the well. It was about noon.

"Let's stop there for a moment and sit down next to Jesus. Imagine the heat of the day. The sun is beating down. You're hot and sweaty. Dust has stuck to your feet and face, becoming muddy as it mixes with the sweat. There's a well where you could get water. It will take some work, but oh, that water would be so refreshing. If only you had a jug to fill.

"Now that you're all looking for your water bottle and wishing it was warmer than it really is today..."

The congregation and Trish laughed.

"Let me ask you this. Why would you wait until noon to draw water when it was hot, and why would you do it alone?"

The questions hung in the air for a minute before Pastor Bennett continued.

"The answer is found in the conversation that we will read. I encourage you to stay seated next to Jesus by that well as a woman who is avoiding rumours and whispers, who is living with shame pressing heavy on her shoulders, and who feels better alone than with people, since no one wants to be associated with her anyway, offers our Saviour a drink of water that will only satisfy for a moment. What she doesn't know is that she will be the one receiving the water of life that day. Let's get back to the text."

Pastor Bennett preached, and Trish drove aimlessly for forty minutes. Finally, as the sermon was drawing to a close, Trish pulled her car to the side of the road. There was an exit up ahead, and she suspected, based on what Pastor Bennett had already said, that her decision to take that exit or continue on this highway would be found in his words.

"Jesus knew this woman's shame," he said. "He even told her about it. And so, too, he knows our shortcomings, our sins, and the ailments that haunt us. While He may expose them to us, did you notice what he did not do? Where do you see His condemnation in this passage? Where do you see Him telling her that she can't be restored? Look carefully. Look at it for days even. You won't find it. It's not there. What is there is an offer of living water, a presentation of Himself as Messiah, and a woman who grabs hold of what He offers and, leaving her water jar, goes to tell others about Him. I'm sure her shame still skulked about in the shadows and was carried on whispers from time to time as it tried to overcome her again.

"But it doesn't. She has been set free. The chains of guilt and shame are broken. While others may try to make her wear her shame again. Jesus never will."

There was a pause and the sound of a Bible closing and shuffling of papers.

"There's one thing I want to say specifically today. It was laid on my heart as I prayed over my notes last night. Therefore, it must be said. We're a family here. The family of God. And as much as I would like to think that no one in this family would ever spread rumours about another family member, I know that we're also all sinners. Redeemed sinners, but sinners none-the-less." Again, he paused before continuing. "I don't know who specifically needs to hear this today, but I would ask that you all hear me well. No condemnation of things that God has pardoned in your lives shall ever fall from my lips. If it does, point it out. Correct me. Help me to live in line with how Jesus lived. What the Lord has set free, is free indeed! Frederick, you can come play for us now."

No condemnation. The words echoed in Trish's mind. She picked up her phone. She needed to find out exactly how far away from home she was.

Messages popped up one after another when she turned the airplane mode off. Henry, Trevor, Lacey, Gran, Brandon – they had all sent her some message that tugged at her heart strings and made her dig her pack of tissues out of her purse. She was loved. Greatly, deeply loved. And nothing, not even herself and her past was going to come between her and that love.

Forty-five minutes back to Hatfield Falls? Wow, that was likely too long to make it back to church before everyone had left.

Where are you? She texted to Henry.

Are you okay?

Yes. Where are you right now?

Church. Brought Trevor back so he could get his van. Where are you?

About forty-five minutes away from church. There's an exit about a kilometer ahead of me. I'm going to turn around there and head back home. To him. She was going home to him.

Henry?

Yes.

Did you tell your dad anything about me and Michael?

No.

How did he know I needed to hear that sermon?

You listened?

I did. Because I thought Gran would want me to.

She would.

How did he know?

He doesn't know. He faithfully preaches, and God does the rest. It was a rather awesome sermon. It really spoke to me. No more hiding.

Yeah, none for me either. Going to drive now.

Be safe. I love you. XO

I will. I love you, too. XO

WAIT! YOU DO? And now mom is looking at me funny. Probably should not have said that out loud. Haha

Yeah, probably best to think texts in your head, Bennett. And yeah, I do. But, I really do have to drive now so I can come home to you.

I like the sounds of that, Beautiful. Meet me at Mom's?

In less than an hour. XO

As Trish turned into the alleyway behind Pastor and Mrs. Bennett's house, she found both Thor and Henry, pacing along the back fence as they waited for her.

"You must be freezing." She reached over the gate to scratch Thor's ear.

"We just came out a few minutes ago, so we're not popsicles yet. Dinner is almost ready, and Mom was thrilled both to hear you were coming and to get the tin of cookies." He opened the gate for her, and once she was through, pulled her into his arms.

"I'm going to tell them," she said as she clung tightly to him. "No more secrets. No more hiding. No more guilt. No more shame. No more condemnation. No more running. I'm home both with you and with God."

"Like you'll marry me, home?"

She unwound her arms from around his waist and slid them up his chest to his face so she could hold his face between her hands. "We'll see when you ask me, but we've only been on two dates."

"I'm asking. Will you marry me? I don't have a ring yet, but I do have several options on my phone that I think look like you, and the jewelry store is open this afternoon."

She laughed. "Just shut up and kiss me. I'll marry you, but please, can we just date for a while first?"

"We can date when we're engaged." He cocked one eyebrow at her in challenge. "I don't want to just say you're my girlfriend. I want to say you're mine, and I'm getting you that ring as soon as possible. Today, if you'll let me."

"I have to tell your parents about Michael today. Can we go tomorrow? I don't have to work."

"Absolutely. I'll take the day off."

"But if you have to work, we can –" She did not get to finish her thought because he cut her off with a kiss that was soft and filled with yearning.

She had been kissed before – by Michael – but none of his kisses had ever been as precious as this one was. Michael's kisses had been demanding and self-seeking. They had never been this gentle. His lips had never caressed hers as if she was a fragile, valuable treasure that needed to be protected.

"We can't wait," Henry whispered between kisses.

His second kiss was just as gentle as his first, but then, it deepened tentatively as if waiting to see how she responded. *She* was his concern even though she could hear his desire in his sigh.

"I won't break," she whispered before she pulled his lips more firmly against hers.

His sigh turned to a groan that was repeated in her soul.

"Oh, hallelujah, the Lord answers prayer!" interrupted their enjoyment of each other.

"Gran, why are you outside? Where's Brandon?" Trish demanded.

Gran grinned, pointed to Trish's left, and said, "Taking pictures. However, I'm getting cold, and my daughter is eager to hear how things stand between you. You are engaged, aren't you?"

"Yes, but I haven't gotten her a ring yet. I had planned to wait a couple more weeks before asking, but..." Henry shrugged and pulled Trish closer to his side as they walked to the house.

"Well, I had hoped you were engaged, or I was going to have to speak to you about how you treat my granddaughter."

"Hey, I'm your grandson."

"You are, and I know how you can be. This one," she motioned to Trish, "needs loving of the best and most respectful kind. She's a treasure."

"Well, then, you have nothing to fear because I couldn't agree more."

"Guess catching the bouquet is a thing," Fred said as he opened the door for Gran.

"Guess it is," Henry agreed. "Maybe you should stand front and center when Trish tosses hers."

Fred laughed. "Nah, not me. I'm too young to be an old married man. Brandon, on the other hand, is getting up there in years."

"Brandon will be holding a camera," Brandon said. "Right? Please say I can take my camera as a date to your wedding and take pictures."

"I'd like that," Trish assured him. "However, you could actually bring a real date and your camera."

"Nope. I don't need a real date. I'm quite happy with my camera."

"Well, then, I guess it's up to Eddie to be next," Frederick said.

"But isn't he the same age as you, and you're too young?" Brandon slipped past Trish and Henry where they stood in the kitchen.

"Well, if you won't take the dive for him, what other option is there? Emma?" Fred laughed all the way to the living room.

"I thought you weren't going to ask her today?" Will teased from where he stood next to a neatly sliced roast.

"I said I wasn't going to ask her today in the foyer. I never mentioned the back yard."

Will chuckled. "I'm happy for you. And Trish, Lacey is patiently waiting to see that you're well. She mentioned something about you knowing Michael?"

"I'll tell you all about that over tea."

"Sounds good."

Trevor stood at the door between the kitchen and dining room. "You're going to tell them?"

Trish nodded. "I want to be free, Trevor."

"Henry mentioned that when he shared your love of today's sermon with his dad." He came over to her and gave her a hug. "I'm glad you're home. Were you really going to leave Hatfield Falls?"

She nodded. "I was thinking about it. I didn't want to, but I didn't know what else to do until I listened to today's sermon. Then, I knew that I'd always be running if I kept clinging to my shame. It's time to let it go." She blew out a breath. "It doesn't mean my heart is completely healed. I still need to figure out what to do about Mom and Dad, but," she twined her fingers with Henry's, "thanks to some rather wonderful people like Lacey, Gran, and Henry, I no longer believe it can't be healed."

"I'm glad to hear it." He tipped his head toward the dining room. "Don't be too long hanging up your stuff in the mud room. I'm starving. May I see you to your seat, Mrs. Green?"

"Mrs. Green?" Gran scoffed. "You'll call me Gran from now on. I've got a lot of grandsons, but that doesn't mean my heart can't hold one more." She patted Trish's arm. "I love you, my dear girl."

"I love you, too, Gran." Trish gave her a quick hug. "I'll be quick."

"Not too quick," Gran whispered. "I think another kiss or two might be good."

"Gran!"

Gran merely chuckled as she let Trevor escort her to the dining room.

"She's right," Henry said as he took Trish's coat from her and hung it up before hanging up his own. "A kiss or two would be very good."

And since Gran was nearly always right, what was a girl to do but kiss the handsome man in front of her? After all, he held her healing heart, which had, through the grace of God and the love of a godly man and his grandmother, found its safe and forever home.

Chapter 20

A Step Towards New Beginnings

The heroine of Hatfield Falls (Don't Tell) Book 3 is Ava, our romance writer, and her romantic hero is Edmund, the fellow who doesn't like romance novels. That should be a fun pairing. Here's a little scene set at the library to help us get to know Ava just a little better.

"What about a book club? That could be fun." Ava looked from Gran to Trish. "I mean, you're going to be a married lady soon, and you won't be part of the singles' group."

"I don't like to read anything unless I picked it. I'm not into homework," Trish said.

Ava crossed her arms and tapped her pen on her upper arm. There had to be some sort of group they could form that would give her a reason to get away from her keyboard and out of the house on a regular basis. "What if we make it a book club without a specific book to discuss?"

"Will it just be us ladies?" Gran asked.

"Well, not just the three of us, but I'm thinking that we're going to talk romance, so probably?"

Gran wrinkled her nose. "Soooooo, no chance of matchmaking then?"

Trish and Ava both laughed. From what Ava had learned in the last two months of occasionally working at the Hatfield Falls library rather than the one in Wilson's Crossing, Gran loved a good romance of the non-book variety.

"We can dish on all the guys we'd like to date – except for Lacey and Trish since that'd be way too much talk about Henry and Will. And we might get a few other married ladies to join us."

"I think all ladies would be nice." Lacey had joined them in the computer room. "Everything is ready for closing. Eddie said he'd watch the front desk so I could join you guys, and Jenna is straightening up the toys in the children's section.

"Am I writing down that this will be a ladies' group?" Ava held her pen poised over her notebook. She liked having plans written down in ink.

"Yes," Trish said as Gran nodded.

"Adult ladies. Married and single. Pick your own book. Anything else?"

"Do we agree it's a once-a-month meeting?" Lacey asked.

"I think that would work best. Maybe the third Thursday of the month? Or should we just pick a day each month for the next month's meeting?" Ava asked.

"I like a schedule."

Trish laughed at Lacey's remark. "And her husband likes schedules even more than she does."

"Routines are relaxing," Lacey protested.

"They are," Ava agreed. She liked familiar patterns that let her brain wander down imaginary paths. "Well, then, if Thursdays work, I can put it down as that for now, and we can revisit the schedule after we've had a few meetings."

"Will this be an outreach or just a fellowship type group?" Trish asked.

"Both," Gran said. "I have a friend at my apartment building who I've been trying to get to come to church with me, but she'll have nothing to do with that. However, she reads several books each week, so I think she'd be willing to come to something that wasn't a Bible study or sermon. I think she needs to see that us churchgoers are just normal folks. So, we'll fellowship around books and reach out to her in the process."

"I like that idea," Trish agreed. "I could have benefitted from something like that when I first arrived in Hatfield Falls."

Ava jotted down what Gran had said as she considered just how strong the rather delicately built Trish Thompson was. "I still can't believe your parents let you leave on Christmas Eve." It was only last month when they had gone out for coffee that Trish had shared her whole story with Ava, and Ava had asked if she could use it as fodder for the plot of a book in the future.

"Yeah, I still struggle with that, too," Trish said. "I'm going to invite them to the wedding, but Trevor is going to walk me down the aisle."

"Your brother is pretty great."

"And single," Gran added.

Ava, Trish, and Lacey all laughed at that.

"I'll keep that in mind," Ava assured Gran. Of course, he wasn't Edmund Bennett, but Trevor Thompson was not only better than average looking, he was also an incredibly sweet man who liked to help where he could. She had only met him a few times, but sometimes you could just tell about some guys. Trevor was one of those guys.

Edmund poked his head into the computer room. "The front door is locked, so you're all going to have to go out the back door, and I'm turning off the lights in five minutes."

Ava closed her notebook. "We just need a name for our book club, but I guess we can message each other with ideas for that."

The others agreed and everyone stood to leave. Ava clicked her messenger bag closed and put the strap over her head.

"What kind of books are you going to read for your book club?" Eddie asked Trish.

"The kind you don't like," she teased.

Edmund shook his head. "Romances?"

"Yes, but there might be other books as well," Lacey said. "It's a read what you want book club."

Edmund's eyebrows rose at that. "How can you discuss a book if not everyone is reading it?"

"How do people leave reviews on retailer sites or Bookbub? Our club will work the same. You pick a book. You read a book. You tell us if you liked it or not and why. And then, we get to ask questions if we want."

"Sounds interesting but not very much like an academic exercise."

"Reading doesn't have to be an academic exercise. In fact, I'd say it is best when it is not done for academic purposes." Ava now stood in front of the fellow she had been admiring from afar for two months. He was even better looking up close, where you could see the flecks of gold in his eyes. "And I would add that people who think all reading must be academic have a rather remarkable tendency to be snobs."

"I am not a snob. I just like to delve deeply into complex stories."

"Ah, and a romance cannot be complex." She swore she saw him lift his chin.

"I didn't say that."

"You didn't have to. It's what a lot of people who haven't read romance think." She lifted a finger. "No, I take that back. They may have read romances, but they haven't read good romances. There's a spectrum of stories ranging from dreadful to delightful in all genres, wouldn't you agree?"

"I suppose." He turned and started walking toward the back of the library where she had seen him entering and exiting frequently. Trish had told her that he spent a good bit of time entering new books into the library's computer system and getting them ready to be put on the shelves.

Apparently, his discussion of romance books with her was over.

"The third Thursday of this month is next week. Are we starting then?" Lacey had her phone in her hand and likely had her calendar open. That girl truly did love schedules and lists.

"I think we should," Gran answered. "I'll get us the community room at my apartment building for the evening, and I'll make cookies."

"And we can all bring our own drink of choice," Trish added.

"If we can find someone to watch Riley, I might be able to bring my sister. She could really use a night out with adults – female adults."

"I'd love to meet her," Gran said.

"I'd love to have her meet all of you." She looked at her phone. "Oh, that's her now. Hey, sis, what do you need me to get on the way home?"

"I... I... I..." There were huge, gulping breaths between the repeated start of her sister's sentence.

"What's wrong?" She grabbed Trish's arm. "She's crying," she mouthed to her.

"I... just need Frank."

"He'll be home in two months."

"No, he won't. Oh, Ava, he's dead."

Ava crouched down close to the ground as the world spun around her. Her brother-in-law was dead? "Have you called Mom and Dad?"

One of the reasons Ali lived in Wilson's Crossing was so she could be close to their parents when her husband was away on deployment.

"No." The word was drawn out and interrupted by sobs. "Ava, what am I going to do?"

"Where's Riley? Is she in bed?" Ava wiped tears from her cheeks with the palm of her hand. Ali and Frank had been in love with each other since grade seven. He was as much a part of her family as any person could ever be, and her sister... oh, what were they going to do without Frank?

"Yes."

"I'll be home as soon as possible, and I'll call Mom before I leave here. I'm on my way. You'll be okay until I get there, right?" She was sitting on the floor now. Trish knelt beside her with a box of tissues.

"I'll never be okay again."

"I know, but I just mean... oh, never mind. Just go curl up in bed, and I'll be there soon."

"Okay."

Ava pulled her phone away from her ear and stared at it. Never had she ever thought she would get a call like that one. These things happened to other people. Not her. She tapped her mom's name, and the phone dialed as Ava put it back to her ear.

One ring. Two rings. Please pick up. Three rings. Please pick up. Four rings.

"Hello, darling." It was how her mom always answered the phone when it was either her or her sister calling.

"Mom, how fast can you get to Ali's place? I'm in Hatfield Falls at the library and about to head home." But her mom was closer.

"I can run over there right now. Why? Is something wrong with her or Riley?"

"It's Frank."

Her mother gasped. "Is he injured?"

"Worse."

"Dead?"

Ava could almost hear her mother searching for a place to sit down.

"Yes. I don't know any details. I just know that she said he was dead." That word was such a dreadful one. So final. So life-altering. It was as if time stood still at the very mention of the word, and no one knew what was going to happen once time began to tick again. "Can you get to her soon?"

"I'll just grab a few things for the night and head right over. Drive carefully. There's no need to rush. I've got this, Ava."

"I love you, Mom."

"I know, and I love you, too."

The phone Ava held went silent.

"Who's Frank?" Edmund asked softly.

"Her sister's husband," Trish answered.

"Oh, my!" Gran cried. "Oh, my! How dreadful."

Ava nodded and rose from the floor to stand on wobbly legs. "I have to get home."

"Are you sure it's safe for you to drive?" Edmund stood at her side, watching her as if he wasn't sure she would stay standing, and truth be told, she wasn't sure she could stay upright for long either.

"What other option is there?" She had to get home, and she wasn't about to call a taxi.

"I can drive you home if you'll trust me to drive your car," Edmund offered. "And maybe Trish or Lacey can follow me, or I can call one of my brothers to come get me and bring me back."

As much as she didn't want to fall apart in front of anyone, especially Edmund, Ava knew from the way her head was spinning and her hands were shaking that driving was not a good idea. "That would be helpful and safest." Her brow furrowed. "I think."

"I'll follow behind you," Lacey said. "Trish is Gran's ride tonight, and I know Henry is expecting her to meet him for pie at the diner."

"Oh, right, I knew about that." Trish and Henry had a pie date at least once a week after Trish got off work.

Edmund put an arm around her shoulder. "Let's get you to your car and home." He gently moved her towards the door. "I'll need your keys." He looked behind him. "Jenna, can you make sure the alarm is set?"

"Of course."

Ava shivered as they walked outside.

"Do you have an emergency blanket in your car?" Edmund asked.

"In the trunk. Why?"

"You should wrap up in it."

He walked with his arm around her shoulder all the way to her car. Then, he stood at her door until she was seated and buckled in before he went to retrieve the blanket from the trunk.

He handed her his phone. "Type in your address and hit start. Then, you don't have to do anything but rest on the way." He closed her door and jogged around to the driver's side where he spent a bit of time adjusting the seat and mirrors to his height.

"Thank you for doing this."

"You're welcome." He put the car into reverse and backed out of the parking spot. Then, he drove to the parking lot entrance and waited until Lacey was behind them.

Ava rested her head against the back of her seat and closed her eyes. Seconds later, or so it seemed, Edmund was pulling into the drive at Ali's house.

"Did I snore?" Ava asked as she checked her chin for drool. Ugh. How could she fall asleep in a car with the guy she'd been crushing on for two months?

"It was more of a soft buzz," he said with a smile. "I'm glad you got some rest. How do you feel?"

"Numb, but not dizzy like I was."

"Good. Can I walk you to the door? Or will that be too much for everyone?"

"I'd like it, but Mom might wonder about why you drove me home, and I'd rather not give her any reason to worry."

"That's perfectly understandable."

Ava climbed out of the car, took her keys back from Edmund, and her bag which he had retrieved from the trunk. She couldn't even remember him taking that from her. It really was a good idea that he had driven her home if she had been so out of it.

"Oh!" she gasped as she felt the weight of her bag in her hand. It was much heavier than it should be if it was just her laptop. "I forgot to give something to Trish." She pulled her soon-to-be-published romance out of her bag. "I promised to let her have an advance copy of my book so she can give me an idea of what reviewers might say."

Edmund's eyes grew wide as he looked at the book. "You're Avery-Anne Johns? We've got several of your books on our shelves at the library."

Oh! What she had just done hit her like her sister's elbow to her belly when she started to tell on her when they were little. "You can't tell anyone this is me." She should have thought of that before showing him the book. Not many knew she wrote romance. There were too many who had "thoughts" about romance and romance writers that she did not want to deal with. Besides, it was much easier to lay your heart on the page when you knew you were anonymous.

"I won't." He flipped the book over and looked at the blurb. "I just had to replace one of your books today because it had been read so many times it was falling apart." He smiled sheepishly at her. "I guess that must mean you're on the good end of the genre spectrum?"

"I'd like to think so, but only you can be the judge of that. Just because I'm good to one reader doesn't mean I'll be good according to all readers."

"This sounds like a pretty good plot."

"Thanks." She stuck her hand back into her bag as an idea struck her. She wasn't sure if it was a good idea or not, but she was going to run with it before her rational brain stopped her. "You know there's one way to find out if I'm good or not. I've got another advance reader copy here if you want it."

"Me? Read romance?" His tone registered his shock at such a notion, but his expression read intrigued.

"I won't tell anyone, and if you find you can tolerate my work, I could use another editor on my list."

"You publish these yourself?"

She nodded and waited for him to tell her that self-publishing was for those who couldn't cut it in the real world of books. However, his look was one of surprise and perhaps admiration? Or was that just her wanting it to be that?

"I promise. I won't tell anyone, and this way, you'll know more about the genre you despise."

"I don't despise..." his words fell away when she cleared her throat. "I will admit that I tend to look down on it." He shifted his weight from one foot to the other.

"Will you read it? Just this one. I won't ask you to read any others unless you want to."

His head bobbed up and down slowly. "Sure. I'll give it a shot, but only if you promise to keep this our secret."

"Deal." She handed him the second copy of her book. "And I want to hear your honest opinion when you're done. If you hate it, tell me, but do it as gently as you took care of me tonight, okay?"

"Okay." He looked from the books he held to Lacey's vehicle.

Ah, yes. How was he going to get those books home without Lacey asking too many questions? Ava reached inside her glove compartment and took out one of her reusable shopping bags. "Here. Use this. It's just a couple of books I asked you to take back to the library, which I have, sort of."

His lips tilted up into an adorable half-smile. "That's brilliant." He stuffed the books in the bag and, after wishing her a good night and offering his condolences, he left.

The reality, which Ava had pushed aside while talking to Eddie about her book, settled around her once again, draping over her like a heavy woolen blanket on a humid summer day. She drew a deep breath, locked her car, and said a quick prayer for strength and wisdom before walking into her sister's house and her life that was forever changed.

Read Ava and Eddie's story in Hatfield Falls (Don't Tell) book 3, *Don't Tell Anyone I Read Romance*, publishing in 2022. Sign up for Annilee's email list for updates on Ava and Eddies story and everything else Hatfield Falls.

About the Author

Annilee Nelson writes faith-filled sweet romances from a cozy corner in the living room of her just-outside-of-Halifax-Nova-Scotia home. She is a life-long lover of stories with her favorite sorts being those that include families, groups of friends, and, of course, romance. Like Mrs. Bennett in the Hatfield Falls series, Annilee loves Jane Austen, though not enough to name her children after Miss Austen's characters.

You can learn more about Annilee, her books, and Nova Scotia (the setting for Hatfield Falls) by signing up for her newsletter at bit.ly/Annilee_Subscribe. You can also find her on Facebook and Mewe and at annileenelson.com.